The Hunger Year

by Lee Conrad Kemsley

BY LEE CONRAD KEMSLEY

The Hunger Year

Published by

Korintok Books

Milton, Vermont 05468

The Hunger Year

Published by KorintokBooks

Cover art by Lorraine Cota Manley
ISBN: 978-0-9913309-0-4

Printed in the United States of America

*To Michael, who gave me the reason to move to Vermont
and to Mae Tao, who gave me the inspiration to write about it.*

Contents

Author's Preface

While I have made every effort to get the historical details correct in this story, this is a work of fiction and is not meant to be an official historic record of this time period. Sackitt's Ridge, Saint Rock, and Tucker Gorge are towns I have imagined, but real towns just like them in Vermont and many parts of New England and Canada experienced unusually cold weather in the spring of 1816—all while trying to recover from the War of 1812 and then the Great September Gale of 1815.

In Vermont, 1815-1816 is still referred to as "1800 and froze to death," or as "the year without a summer." A snowstorm in early June dropped more than a foot of snow in temperatures that were well below freezing. June, July, and August all had killing frosts accompanied by drought. The sheep had already been sheared when the coldest of the summer temperatures occurred, and the hard frosts soon affected the growing season. This was a time when heroes were made from hardscrabble, careworn farmers—and, tragically, when some families at the end of their rope committed suicide to avoid starvation.

Unbeknownst to most New Englanders at the time, drastically unusual weather patterns were occurring in parts of North Africa, the Ottoman Empire, Switzerland, Italy, and western Europe and were also followed by catastrophic crop failures. According to our modern-day studies of weather patterns we now know this period of freakish weather was the direct result of a volcanic eruption on Mount Tambora in Indonesia. It resulted in one of the worst famines of the nineteenth century.

What happened with the weather during this time has become a part of Vermont legend, but I also used as reference David Ludlum's *New England Weather Book* and *The Vermont Weather Book*, and Brian Fagan's *The Little Ice Age—How Climate Made History 1300-1850*. A condensed list of excellent resource books I used in researching the culture of this time period can be found in the back of this book.

I've always worried that historical fiction has the potential, if gotten wrong, to skew our knowledge of history. But what I came to believe in writing *The Hunger Year* is that perhaps fiction writers can help imagine the people who might have lived during the times where the records can no longer help us. Our stories and imaginations can help fill in the blanks and perhaps allow us a better understanding of the strength and fortitude many of those people must have had to survive.

—*Lee Conrad Kemsley*

Chapter 1

The Pest House

Pulling the thin moth-eaten blanket up around her chin for the little warmth it offered, seventeen-year-old Magen Creed tried to comfortably fit her long, graceful frame in the pest-house cot that was the same size for every patient—too short.

She devised schemes in her head to prevent the "bone chopper" from making his way toward her sister Carrie's bed to bleed her again."Bleeding them is all we can do," the grizzled old physician had told Sara, Magen's stepmother, when she came to visit them at the pest house that morning. Carrie had been too weak to sit up to receive her mother's kiss, and Sara did not offer Magen one.

"You don't look as bad as Carrie. Are they giving you something she's not getting?" Sara asked Magen as she nervously stared at the fever victims. Magen could not think of a response, but it didn't matter. Sara had already turned to leave, saying she would try and come again, but that "it was hard to get loan of the buckboard."

Magen wondered if she and Carrie would be alive the next time Sara made it to the pest house. Two days ago it had been Lucas, a ten-year-old boy lying next to her, who died. Lucas was the one who had nicknamed the doc the "bone chopper." He had been looking at Magen, not saying anything, just watching her. That horrible rattle rocked his sunken chest. And then the light just left his eyes. Magen had been kind to Lucas as she was to everyone, and he had tried to tell her funny stories to keep her spirits up.

Straining to decipher the rasp of her young stepsister's breathing from that of the others, Magen cursed the pest-house warden under her breath. He was too parsimonious to leave even a single candle burning for them to see by, but then used so much lye to scrub the floors that their eyes and throats constantly burned.

"Carrie," Magen whispered, only to be groaned at by the old lady who lay between them. Carrie gave no reply, and Magen could just barely make out her younger sister's mop of blonde curls in the dark. Magen remembered how Carrie would sit patiently while Sara tied up her wavy yellow hair with wet strips of cotton. Then Carrie would ask Magen to sit still while she tried to create the same curls in Magen's long, thick, raven-colored hair.

"Why is your hair so different, Magey?" Carrie would ask. And Sara was always quicker than Magen with a response: "Because she's a Creed, Carrie. And all the Creeds have hair like that."

"I like the way it shines when I brush it," Carrie would whisper to Magen out of Sara's hearing. So Magen would make herself sit still while Carrie painstakingly braided her straight hair into one single plait that hung down her back. It didn't bother Magen that her hair could not hold the stylish curls, what mattered was that Carrie liked the way it looked.

Trying to count the number of days they had been in the pest house now, Magen remembered it had started the night of Carrie's seventh birthday. It was a special evening with food and laughter. Sara had baked a special brown betty in honor of the day, and Miss Wordleave, their neighbor, had brought extra maple sugar to crumble on top. They sang songs, and even Sara laughed and danced part of an Irish jig.

But when Magen woke the next morning she knew something was wrong. She heard Carrie whimpering like a sick puppy. Magen tried to get up and go to Carrie, and that's when she realized she felt bad herself—weak and aching. By that evening they both had raging fevers, and Carrie had a cough that ripped through her chest. Sara, as always, was frantic and did not know how to cope alone.

"It's the Genessee fever, Sara! You know that it is," was Miss Wordleave's pronouncement. Magen shuddered to hear it. "You'll have to take them to the pest house on the other side of the settlement. They'll be seen by a physician there," Miss Wordleave assured Sara—as if the pest house was a good thing. Magen knew those who didn't survive the pest house would be carted away.

"It's always the people who are fightin' to survive as it is that gets hit the hardest," Miss Wordleave continued, trying to sound sympathetic to Sara's plight. Magen believed that was true enough. The consequences of the war that had started in 1812 had hit their corner of New York hard. Sackitt's Ridge was a small settlement made up of poor tenant farmers who had been made poorer by the times. It was the war that had caused her Pa, Samuel, to leave. But the Treaty at Ghent signed on Christmas Eve in 1814 ended the war. Yet in this year of 1815 the fever persisted.

2

Sara had finally capitulated and then had to beg their more wealthy neighbor, Jeb Shepard, to loan her his buckboard to take the girls to the pest house. Like everyone else, he was afraid of catching the fever and would not go. Yet he allowed Sara to borrow the wagon and take the girls herself. It had probably been eleven days ago now.

Although Magen was not as sick as Carrie, everyone who was sent to the pest house was placed together in one long dormitory room. As Magen kept a strained eye on her sister's cot, she saw one of the night wardens move the man from the cot to the left of Carrie's. Magen quickly picked up her blanket and moved herself into the vacant spot next to Carrie's.

Magen felt protective of her younger half-sister. Carrie was short, fair, and plump like Sara, whereas Magen was tall and slender like her Pa. Looking at Carrie in the pest house cot, Magen regretted all the times she had complained about having to do Carrie's chores; it occurred to her that what she really regretted was that Carrie had a mother who loved her and Magen did not.

Magen was a lot like her father Samuel, who stayed away from their cheerless home as much as possible. She had learned at a young age how to be alone, until eventually she grew to love her solitude. She passed many an afternoon trekking through their corner of the Adirondack mountains, spending long hours in the forest examining plants, spying on the wildlife, and investigating the terrain near their cabin home. The natural world made sense to her. She could see how it worked, and she felt a part of it. People were much more difficult to understand.

Leaning in close to Carrie's ear, Magen now whispered, "Pa will be returning soon from Canada, Carrie. With the money he earned from smuggling, maybe we'll go to Vermont where he grew up and buy our own farm. You've got to get better so we can help him build it into a fine place." Samuel had been gone for more than two years now, smuggling ponies to the British troops across the border in Canada. It wasn't being a traitor if it was done to keep your family alive, Magen told herself. When the war ended, trade with Canada resumed and things were just starting to get better for folks, but still Samuel Creed did not return.

Magen reached out to lightly hold Carrie's delicate hand. Carrie's skin looked almost translucent, especially next to her own sun-browned skin. Magen remembered her father once saying that Sara and Carrie "were a world unto themselves." Instinctively, Magen knew what he meant.

Carrie's chills shook the rickety cot. Her moans sounded primal. Fearing Carrie's thrashing would segue into one of those relentless coughing spells, Magen dipped a strip of muslin cloth in a bowl that sat on the table next to the bed. The bowl was full of pulverized inner bark from the slippery elm tree steeped in water, and Magen used the soaked muslin to attempt to cool Carrie's hot skin.

Carrie felt like little more than a bird to Magen as she held her sister's head up. Since coming to the pest house, the two sisters had been fed only small amounts of dried bread and potatoes in attempt to starve the fever. Magen was certain this restricted diet had the opposite effect and decided to try and find Carrie more food. She left Carrie's cot and tiptoed into the back room larder. If it hadn't been for the moonlight shining through the windows she wouldn't have been able to see at all. She grabbed some stale bread and what she hoped was a slice of dried beef.

She crept back to Carrie with the small bit of food. As she sat down next to her, Magen noted the silence and then the stillness of her fingers. She turned Carrie's face toward her and knew in an instant that Carrie was gone. In just the time it had taken Magen to go to the larder, Carrie's thrashing had stopped and she was at peace. *How curious and difficult life was to understand*, she thought, hugging Carrie's body. She was too weak to shed real tears—but inside her head, Magen wailed.

Chapter 2
Ashes to Ashes

It had been a night and most of a day since Carrie had died. Her body lay on the cot next to Magen's, wrapped in a soiled linen that covered her face. Magen wouldn't look at it. Mostly she kept her eyes closed tight or stared out the one small window that faced the only road to this desolate place. She was the first to spot the horse and wagon as it plodded down the road. Her heart fluttered when she realized it was Sara, and in an instant, she thought—*Escape!*

Throwing off her own sheet, Magen was at the door in the outer vestibule when Sara walked through it in a trance. Magen tried to prevent her from seeing Carrie's body. But Sara was on a mission and Magen was not part of it. Speaking aloud to no one in particular, Sara said "I'm taking my child."

Magen, frantic that she was going to be left behind, grabbed her homespun smock and thin leather flats from under the bed pad. She was dressed and assisting Sara with Carrie's body before the matron was even aware of Sara's arrival.

"We take care of the dead bodies here, ma'am," the caretaker insisted as she hurried in from the other room. "It's safer that way."

Magen knew Sara was incapable of talk just now, so she said with all the authority she could muster: "We're taking my sister home." Without waiting for the argument that she knew would come, Magen lifted Carrie's wrapped body from Sara's arms and went out and laid her in the back of the wagon. Then she assisted Sara up onto the buckboard, settled her with the reins, and climbed in back with Carrie. All the while, Magen tried hard not to cough or throw up or look in any way like she should not be leaving the pest house. Sara snapped the reins and they left without a backward glance.

Magen knew they had been lucky. If the warden or physician or anyone else with real authority had been there, they would not have been allowed to leave. Holding onto her sister's corpse so it wouldn't roll back and forth,

Magen closed her eyes and thanked God for giving her the strength to carry her sister's body to the wagon. She had always been strong, and had a memory of helping her Pa load groceries into a wagon years ago. She could hear her Pa's voice saying "Magen has my strength but her Ma's good looks." It was one of the rare times he had ever mentioned Magen's real mother, Ruth. Sarah didn't like talk of Ruth, so all Magen knew of her was that she had long dark hair and golden skin.

As the buckboard made its mournful journey back to Sackitt's Ridge, Magen drank in the cool mountain air whipping around her face. Although it made her feel guilty, Magen felt glad to be alive. By the time they reached their cabin, it was late afternoon. Magen felt as weak as a sick lamb, but she knew her fever had broken. She pulled herself out of the wagon and met Sara's eyes. Each had noticed that both Jeb Shepard and Miss Wordleave were standing with the village squire in front of their cabin door. Miss Wordleave stopped just short of approaching them.

"The squire here told us of your loss, Sara, and we're sorry. But you shouldn't have brought Carrie's body back with you."

"We can't chance spreadin' the sickness here, Mrs. Creed," the squire chimed in. "We've arranged for the body in the back, and it's best we deal with it right now."

Sara stood mute. Magen stumbled past her to the back of the house and saw where they had dug a pit downwind from where the cabins were clustered. A bed of wooden slats surrounded by dry limbs was waiting for its sole final occupant. Mustering what little strength she had left, Magen turned to the tiny group of neighbors and told them to leave—she would do what had to be done. Miss Wordleave and the squire, skittish about being around anyone who had the sickness, backed away and headed down the path. Jeb Shepard stood his ground and the squire nodded to him, grateful to turn over the distasteful job that was to come. Magen wasted no time in assisting Sara into the cabin. When she came back outside she held a torch she had made from the fire in the hearth. She headed toward the wagon and Carrie's body.

Jeb surprised Magen then by reaching out to put his hand on her shoulder. "Let me put Carrie's body in the burn pit, Magen." With a gentleness Magen had only ever witnessed in animals, the lumbering bulk of old Jeb Shepard, with his rough, calloused hands, lifted the body from the wagon and carried it over to the altar of wood. He tenderly placed it on top of the dry boughs. With an unsteady hand, Magen bent down and lit Carrie's funeral pyre.

Magen and Jeb Shepard stood like wooden statues as the white hot flames consumed Carrie's small body. They could hear Sara weeping inside the cabin. They stood silently until the fire depleted itself. Magen had known real loss when her father left, and had grown up with the loss of her own mother. But until this moment, the chasm between life and death—the invisible divide between this world and the next—had never seemed so real to her, nor so tenuous.

Later that night, both exhausted, Magen and Sara lay on their cots in front of the small kitchen hearth. Sara had said very little in the hours since their departure from the pest house, and she hadn't eaten any of the meager supper that Magen had prepared. She didn't ask Magen how she felt, nor did she communicate in any way about the events of the afternoon.

As the fire warmed the damp, chilly cabin, Magen listened as the sounds of Sara's muffled crying joined the night noises: the mountain breeze pushing against the creaking frame of the wooden cabin and the coyote's distant howl. Tired as she was, Magen's mind raced with a tangle of emotions all vying for her attention—grief at the loss of Carrie, gratitude that the fever hadn't gotten her, and intense relief to be out of the pest house. She attributed her survival to what her father used to call "that hard-headed Creed constitution." Magen made a conscious choice then and there that she would never take her life for granted again. But the very next thought that presented itself in her exhausted head was, *what now?*

Chapter 3
The Decision

The trade embargoes with Canada and the war against Britain in 1812 had hit everyone in the young country of America hard but especially the already-strapped people of Sackitt's Ridge. "The land was bad on the Ridge," people would say. Samuel Creed said it was the people's attitude toward the land that was the real problem.

Magen knew her father and her grandfather, Silas Creed, had had a falling out. Her grandfather had been a preacher—a "circuit rider" for a time. She thought that had sounded like a noble life, but her Pa had said nobility had nothing to do with it. She never received much more of the story.

Before he left for Canada, Samuel had left Magen a small leather map. She knew it showed the way to the Creed family farm in the Champlain Valley of Vermont, but Pa had not explained why he was giving it to her. The morning after her return from the pest house, the map popped into Magen's head as she was milking their sullen cow. She looked around her at the withered crops and the meager store of dried food. She knew that the supply of candles in the pantry wouldn't last the month and the firewood had not been cut for the winter season. Perhaps her father had left her the map for a reason; perhaps it was her only hope.

Magen marched back into the cabin and found Sara staring out the window. "Sara," she announced. "We can't stay here any longer."

Sara didn't shift her gaze.

"Our only hope is to pack up and head out," Magen insisted. She wondered nervously if she would be able, after all, to convince Sara to leave.

Sara finally responded in a dull voice. "Are you daft? Where would we go?"

"The Creed Farm. My grandparents' farm. It's just over the lake in Vermont." Magen moved herself between Sara and the window so that her stepmother would be forced to look at her. "We'll never survive here like this," she said, waving her hand to encompass the barren room and the unhappiness that filled it.

Sara's face softened for just a moment and then hardened again. "Has the fever unhinged you? Where did you get such a foolish idea?"

Magen handed Sara the leather map. "I wanted to show you this before I go and ask Jeb Shepard if he'll sell us his wagon." Sara turned the leather strip over in her hands as Magen continued. "Pa left it to me just before he took off for Canada. It's where he came from in Vermont. He never said why exactly, but I think he left me this map so that we would one day go there. He knew he had too much pride to go back home. But I think he would have wanted us to go there if he didn't come back."

"We don't even know if the Creed farm is still there. We don't know anything about it," Sara said.

"It can't be such a great distance. And if it's still there, we can both help work it," Magen continued. She moved toward the hearth and loosened a floorboard near the side of it. From inside the hole in the floor Magen pulled out a jam jar half-filled with various coins. Her Pa had explained once that ever since the confusion of the war, some merchants in New York still used the English system of pence and shillings; the merchants where Magen was hoping to head might use anything from Russian kopecks to the silver dollars they mint in Mexico. Breathless now, Magen shook the jar of coins. "I'm not sure what these coins are or how much they're worth. But it is all we have and I'm sure we'll need to pay our way at some point."

Sara stood up then, and started gathering items from around the cabin. Magen allowed herself a tiny smile as she added the coin jar to the pile of pots and pans already collected.

"Not much to show for our years of struggle here, is it?" Sara asked.

"But you're a good cook, Sara, and I'm a strong worker. Pa had only one sister and his parents would be old now if they're even alive. I'm sure they will welcome our help. We'll be there long before winter begins in earnest." Magen said it as if the matter had been settled. She knew Sara was not up to any sustained argument, so she quickly took charge and rattled off instructions before Sara could change her mind.

"I am going to go and talk to Jeb Shepard about accepting our cow for his wagon. Pinetop is a strong enough horse to get us there if we have a wagon. You gather our warmest clothes, and Pa's woolen trousers, too. We can tie our hair up in Pa's caps so we won't be recognized as women. We'll take the back logging roads, and we won't be dawdling along the way. You'll see Sara, we'll be there in no time!"

Magen took the shortcut through the woods to Jeb Shepard's cabin and it occurred to her that she would be leaving these woods, possibly forever. All she knew of the world was here. Her Pa had taught her the names of all the trees and wildflowers for miles around. She had hiked the hills here in every season. But to stay meant certain death; she was sure of that. And she didn't survive that horrible fever only to die from starvation in Sackitt's Ridge. This is what her Pa would want. When he finally makes it back from Canada, Magen told herself, Jeb Shepard would tell him where they had gone.

Chapter 4

Departure

It took less than a couple of hours to pack up their belongings and to see to their holdings, such as they were. Magen had made the swap—their cow for Shepard's wagon. Luckily, they had the beautiful dappled-gray horse Jeb Shepard had given Carrie as a gift. She had named him Pinetop because when she rode him she felt like she was among the treetops. He was an old horse, but it had been a generous gift. Jeb Shepard had always had a soft-spot for Carrie.

Sara and Magen said their goodbyes to Miss Wordleave, who was unhappy to hear about their departure. By losing Sara, she would be losing the only woman in Sackitt's Ridge who could stand her company. Yet Magen could sense the woman's eagerness for them to be off so that she could be the first to tell the other neighbors of Sara's foolish decision to go to Vermont. Magen had always thought Miss Wordleave's name suited her as no other could. She always had to have the last word.

Magen didn't let on to Sara how dangerous she thought the journey might possibly be. *Two women alone in the wilderness?* It wasn't the distance they had to cross, so much as the wildness of the country. Outwardly, though, Magen never wavered, and soon the horse and wagon trudged out of Sackitt's Ridge with the two women's meager belongings.

Magen usually walked Pinetop by the reins while Sara walked behind the wagon, making sure they were all of a piece. Sara's melancholy had turned into a general irritation now—sometimes directed at Magen, sometimes at the horse. One morning when Sara was taking her turn at the front of the wagon with the reins, Pinetop helped to change the mood. For every complaint Sara lodged against Pinetop as they loped along, the old horse would lodge one right back by nudging Sara ever so slightly with his head. Sara finally had to laugh when Magen, having watched from behind, yelled out "He understands every word you say, Sara." For a while after that things were blessedly quiet.

Along their route they passed all that was familiar to Magen—even the one-room schoolhouse Magen had attended up until two years ago. Later, as she plodded alongside Pinetop at the front of the wagon, Magen shared her feelings about the magic these woods had always held for her. Sara didn't show the least bit of interest. Still, Magen told her about where she searched for the first heal-all and honeysuckle of the season, and where she marked out the purple flowering thimbleberries so she could go pack to pick them when they ripened. She called out other names of flowers that grew along the forest floor, such as the scarlet lobelia and the Jack-in-the-pulpits.

"Carrie and I used to squeeze the red liquid from the roots of the bloodroot flowers and paint our faces like Indians going off to battle," Magen remembered aloud. The mention of Carrie stirred something in Sara's awareness, but it soon vanished. "I know you'll think me odd, Sara, but I used to name all the trees around our cabin. There was one tree in particular, a giant gnarly maple that had a huge limb I could climb into and read my book."

Magen remembered the time she overheard Sara tell a neighbor that Magen was "of different blood." She had sat in her maple tree contemplating this for so long that she had fallen asleep one afternoon. She didn't wake up until long past dark, and then had to make her way back to the cabin in the pitch black. Sitting in front of the fire with her crocheting, Sara had not noticed her absence, nor her return. Magen remembered thinking at the time, *this is what it means to be of different blood.* It was then that she had decided that she had sap in her veins, instead of blood. And that this had made her a true sister to the trees.

Chapter 5
Sara's Journey Ends

Days passed as the old wagon lumbered along craggy clods of dirt and rock. Pinetop would snort and shake his head to show his displeasure. He wasn't used to pulling heavy loads across such difficult terrain. And even though Magen knew she had survived the worst of the fever, she did not have her full strength back. Her legs wobbled, and sometimes she found herself shaking. But she wouldn't complain to Sara.

She didn't think it would take much to set Sara off just now. Since Carrie's death, Magen noticed a wild look that would sometimes come into Sara's eyes; it reminded her of a caged animal.

Sara and Magen fell into an unspoken rhythm. The paths they followed through the mountain were lined by tall indian grass and milkweed on either side. The trail was rocky, sometimes muddy. Because of the wagon, their pace was slow and measured. The mosquitoes and black flies were vicious. Magen tried to talk to Sara about Creed Farm and to encourage her to imagine their futures there. But it was clear Sara didn't see this as the beginning of a new life, because she couldn't see past the one that had just ended—Carrie's.

For the past day and a half they had been traveling on a treacherous stretch of an old military road. Even though the war was over, small groups of militiamen passed now and then, unconcerned and indifferent to their presence. They were high up in the Adirondack mountains, this part of the narrow pass full of ruts. Planting one foot down, then another, Magen did not want to let a foot slip that might cause Pinetop to falter on the precarious passageway. She trembled as she inspected the sharp drop-off on either side of the wagon.

"Walk on, horse! Walk on!" Sara urged impatiently from atop the wagon seat. The horse's head reared back every time she snapped the reins.

Suddenly the wagon lurched. Pinetop stumbled. Sara jerked her side of the harness with both hands, while an agitated Pinetop stopped midtrail.

Magen looked behind her at the wagon and could see the rear axle stuck in a rut. They had scarcely enough room to maneuver.

Sara scrambled down off the wagon and cut a thorny bough from a nearby bush. "Move on you stubborn mule!" she yelled as she whipped it across Pinetop's back. But Pinetop could do nothing. He began to skitter with a look of panic in his eyes.

"Whoa boy. It's all right, stay calm" Magen tried to reassure him. It was obvious the left rear wagon wheel had sunk too far down into the mud on the narrow path. All their worldly goods and the wagon were sitting at an awkward angle to the road. Magen knew Pinetop would not have the strength to pull it out. "We can dig our way out, Sara. I'll get the shovel. Just hold on!"

Scrambling into the wagon Magen managed to find an old gardening spade in the heap of disarray. She and Sara took turns digging around the rear wheel. The handle on the spade broke off before they were finished. Using their hands and rocks, they tried scooping the dirt and mud away from the hub. Finally, they dug enough to clear the wheel.

"Magen, go pull the lead rope while I push on the wheel from back here!" Sara ordered. Magen ran up to the front of the wagon. Jerking hard on Pinetop's rope, she leaned into the road and pulled with all of her strength. "Harder! Pull harder!" Sara yelled again from behind.

Magen felt a brief give in the rope's tension, but just as quickly, Pinetop stumbled and the wagon rolled backward. Magen heard a horrible crunch and then a gagging sound from Sara. Looking back, she saw Sara pinned up to her chest underneath the wheel. Her body wasn't moving. Panicked, Magen gave one more herculean pull on Pinetop's lead before the wagon lunged forward once more. With trembling hands, Magen wound the reins around the brake lever.

"Sara! Sara!" Magen called as she picked her way along the narrow passageway to the back of the wagon. Arriving there, Magen stood motionless. She was numb with terror; she could neither move nor talk.

The weight of the wagon had been cleared from Sara's chest with Pinetop's final pull, but her body lay broken by the wheel. Magen knelt down by her side. Holding Sara's head in her lap Magen murmered, "Sara. I'm so sorry. Can you speak?"

After a moment, Sara began to moan. "Leave it, girl. Just leave it," she rasped.

Panic was rising in Magen's throat. "You have to get up, Sara! I can fix you. But you have to try! You can't die and leave me all alone!"

As Magen held her stepmother's head up, blood spilled from Sara's mouth and the life left her body. Magen's cries sounded for all the world like a wounded bear cub. Feeling the familiar coldness taking over Sara's body, Magen held her like she once held Carrie. Only this time there was no one else around.

Chapter 6
Alone

Magen woke to the pale dawning of the early morning light. She didn't know how long she had been lying next to Sara's cold, stiff body on the trail. Everything felt unreal, and she couldn't bring herself to look at Sara's face. Pinetop was snorting, agitated. Covered with mud and blood, Magen's face was swollen with tears and exhaustion.

Trying to keep her panic from overtaking her, she got up to look for the shovel they had used on the wheel. Not allowing herself to think about what she was doing, she started to dig a grave with the broken shovel. The hard, uneven ground made it more difficult than Magen imagined it could be. But she knew she would never be able to lift Sara into the wagon, so she continued with the unrelenting task.

Eventually she managed a hole large enough for a body. Gritting her teeth, she leaned up and rolled Sara's body into it. But the body landed face down in the grave and Magen knew that was wrong. She tried to turn her over. Frustrated and on the edge of hysteria, Magen was incapable of turning her more than partially over. She covered Sara as best she could with dirt, rocks, and branches from the path. Standing there trying to think, Magen tried to recite one of the prayers she had heard in church, but couldn't remember all the words. So her eulogy was simple: "Sara, Carrie, maybe you're both together now. If so, take care of each other…and maybe Pa and I will see you by and by." In the face of all this death, Magen couldn't help fanning the small kernel of hope in her heart that her Pa was still alive somewhere.

Her arms ached. She put the broken shovel away and tried to settle Pinetop's skittishness. He was an intelligent horse and he sensed Magen's fear, as she sensed his. With effort, she started to lead him and the wagon away from the grave site. *One foot in front of the other… one foot in front of the other.*

She felt sick that she had abandoned Sara on that lonely hillside. *Or was it Sara that had abandoned her?* She wasn't sure that it mattered now. She was alone. She forced herself to maintain a slow pace, leading Pinetop and the rickety wagon down the rocky ravine. She couldn't seem to complete a simple thought, so she just continued to move her body. She focused on listening to her breath in sync with that of the horse's. She knew she should report Sara's death—but to whom? and where? Aside from those few soldiers she saw in the distance the other day, she had not passed another living soul. She considered returning to Sackitt's Ridge, but she didn't consider this for long. Whatever was going to become of her, going backward was not an option.

Nothing had changed, she reassured herself. Inspecting her father's thinning leather map—as she often did when feeling afraid—Magen could make out a small circle midway between New York and the town of Saint Rock in Vermont. The circle had been burned in and had a tiny cross at the center of it. Magen knew her father was not a religious man, and she wondered why he would have marked that place with a circle and a cross. Was it a settlement of some kind? A church?

After miles more of hard walking, Magen guided Pinetop off the path and pulled the wagon underneath a birch grove just as the sun was beginning to set. As she bedded Pinetop and then herself down for a night of well-deserved sleep, niggling doubts began to creep into her mind. *What if Creed Farm no longer existed? And what if her relatives didn't want her to stay? Who would know or care if she never made it to Vermont at all?*

Exhausted, but too keyed up to sleep, Magen laid there waiting for the dark to wrap itself around her. Every muscle ached and her feet throbbed. She thought about Sara and wondered if she had at last found peace. She tried to imagine her father gazing up at the same brilliant night sky she now contemplated.

The giant trees surrounding the wagon looked as though they were watching over her with bent heads. *My old friends*, she thought. It wasn't difficult now to pretend that the great tall oaks and hemlocks surrounding her were relatives of the gentle giants she had known in Sackitt's Ridge. Somehow they knew her, and were keeping sentry duty around her campsite.

Chapter 7
Discovering the Past

In the morning, Magen was anxious to be off. She gave Pinetop a bit of grain and let him drink from the creek before she hitched him to the wagon and started moving them onward. It was past noon when she and Pinetop came to a clearing in the passage. The dark shelter of the evergreens ended, and Magen felt a lightening of her spirit. She could just make out a cabin ahead, framed by white birches with their rustling leaves already turning yellow. She was sure this was the spot marked by a circle and a cross on her father's map.

Studying the cabin up on the rise as she and Pinetop approached it, she saw smoke trickling from its chimney. Her mouth watered as she imagined a hot bowl of stew. As she got closer, she felt giddy at the sight of purple aster growing in front of the house, just like back home. She realized how starved she was for a bit of human company.

"Surely anyone who lives in this cheerful looking place would welcome us, Pinetop," she said aloud. Then she spotted a woman behind the cabin working in a garden. She pulled Pinetop over with a soft "whoa" and tied him off on a limb. The woman noticed her and stopped her gardening.

"We don't get many strangers in these parts, young man," the woman called out to Magen. Her hand was cupped over her brow to block the sunlight.

Magen stopped and yanked her cap off.

"Oh my! Not a young man at all, I see. It's a very pretty lady under all that dirt," said the woman, this time with a smile in her voice.

"I—I—I've come from Sackitt's Ridge, ma'am," Magen stammered as the woman slowly approached. "I'm on my way to my family's farm across the lake in Vermont. And this place, you see, appears to be marked on my father's map." Magen pointed to the circle and cross on the map.

The woman glanced at it, then examined Magen. "I see," she said. "Well, where is your father, child? And the rest of your people?" She was gazing past Magen as if expecting someone else to appear from behind the wagon.

"I am alone, ma'am. My stepmother was with me, but there was an accident." Magen felt the strangeness of the words. This was more difficult than she imagined it would be. Tears started to fill her deep brown eyes and she was embarassed. This won't do, she thought, and she stopped talking.

The woman approached Magen with a look of concern in her eyes. "Dear child, you come in the house with me. You look all done in. This is Abraham Able's home. I'm his wife, Sophia."

Magen had to turn away from the kindness she saw in the old woman's eyes for fear of blubbering. She followed the woman through the back door of the cabin. The home was sparsely furnished but tidy, and the wide-planked pine floor gave off a sweet smell of beeswax. A heavy maple trestle table sat in the center of the largest room next to a crackling fireplace.

Magen looked in one of the smaller side rooms as she passed it. A beautiful red and yellow patchwork quilt lay across the bed. On a side table with a washbowl and pitcher, a small cup contained a few lupine along with some of the asters Magen had admired out front. As they entered the large kitchen, Sophia Able emptied her apron of a pile of string beans; Magen hadn't even noticed she had been carrying them. "The last of the late summer beans," Sophia sighed. "You sit down here, and I'll make us some tea."

Magen did as instructed. She watched the woman gathering the items for tea, and heard heavy footsteps out on the front stoop.

"Must be my man's home to eat," Sophia said, continuing her preparations. "He has his smithy just down the road a bit." Just as the words left Sophia's mouth, the front door opened to reveal a giant of a man. His long black beard was streaked with gray, and the heavy leather apron he wore touched the top of a pair of buckskin moccasins that were bound around his enormous legs with rope.

He entered the house and in a booming voice, declared, "Wife, I'm hungry for my dinner." Smiling, Sophia turned to the man and gestured toward Magen.

"We have a guest, Bram. Our young friend has just arrived from over in Sackitt's Ridge. I'm preparing our tea while we hear what she has to tell us. Sit, husband."

The man looked at Magen with undisguised curiosity and lowered his great frame onto the wooden bench across from her. Magen noticed tiny black lines of soot on either side of his crinkled eyes. He seemed to have soot in every crease of his skin. Magen had never seen such powerful hands, nor such black ones.

"You're alone?" he asked. Magen nodded. "Hm. Let's hear your story then, child."

Magen gathered her thoughts, took a deep breath, and began. "My sister was taken by the fever. Then my stepmother was crushed by the wagon wheel along the logger's trail not three days ride from here," she rushed through in a shaky voice. This time she managed to continue. "I am following a map that my father left me to find the Creed family farm in Vermont. You see," she said showing the map to the great bulk of a man this time, "there's a circle with a cross marked just here where your settlement is." Bram took the map and began to study it as Magen continued. "I wanted to inform someone about what happened to my stepmother and where I buried her along the trail. From the markings my Pa made on his map, it looked as though maybe I was meant to stop here."

When she got no reaction from the Ables, Magen kept going, "I didn't give Sara much of a burial. Only did the best that I could. But I would feel better knowing someone else knew of where I left the grave." She stopped then and caught her breath, trying to gauge their reactions.

"Law sakes, child! What an awful time you have had. You must be very brave," Sophia said with such tenderness that Magen felt the tears prick at the back of her eyes.

"Tell us your name again?" Bram asked.

"I am Magen Creed. We followed the militia and the logging roads across the mountains, Sara and I. Avoiding strangers as best we could. We had no choice but to be traveling without an escort, foolish as it may seem. But not so great a distance, we thought."

"Your family name is Creed, you say? Who is your father and how is it he lets his wife and young daughter wander the countryside alone?" Bram's voice boomed, while Sophia nudged him to soften his query.

"My father is Samuel Creed. He went north to Canada two years and some months since, sir, and he hasn't returned. My stepmother believed him to be dead. But of this I am not certain."

"You're bound for Vermont, you say?" Sophia asked.

"Yes. My father's family has a farm just across the lake near a place called Saint Rock. That's where I'm headed."

"Your real mother, child. What was her name?" Sophia inquired.

Surprised by the question, Magen hesitated. "Why, Ruth, ma'am. My mother's name was Ruth. I wasn't but a babe when she died. So I don't remember her."

Bram looked over at his wife and then pointed to Magen's map. Magen saw plainly that the map and the answers she had given had meant something to them, but she couldn't imagine what that was. Sophia came over to her with a look of incredulity in her eyes. She placed her wrinkled hand on Magen's shoulder and paused for a moment before she spoke.

"A number of years ago," she began, "a young man and his wife were journeying west. They stopped here in need of help, as our cabin was one of the very few built here then. The wife was faring poorly. They had their small child with them, just a baby she was. Of course we did what we could. But by that evening the young woman was delirious with fever. Within but a day's time she was gone." Sophia's voice trailed off, assessing Magen's reaction. After a moment she continued: "Her name was Ruth, dear. I believe she was your mother."

Sophia looked up at her husband for confirmation, and the big man said, "His name was Samuel. He was leaving his home because he couldn't get along with his Pa. I thought he was making a mistake and I told him so. So you are that little babe? Now on an adventure of her own," he concluded in amazement.

"Think of it!" Sophia exclaimed. "To come full circle like that. The angels have been keeping an eye on you, I should think. Making your way back here, all on your own!"

"Easy now, mother," Bram said, trying to sound calm despite an edge of disbelief in his own voice. "We're that sorry your Pa isn't with you, child," he said, considering the events of Samuel's journey so many years ago. "He never made it out of New York, then?"

Magen sat stunned. She tried to assimilate these revelations with what little she knew, or thought she knew about her real mother. She hadn't known where her mother had died; her Pa had so rarely spoken of her.

"Your Pa was awful broken up over losing your Ma," Sophia now reminisced. "He stayed with us for a bit—the both of you did. You were such a sweet baby, not even a year old. Your dark brown eyes so big and thoughtful-like. Quiet though. I remember thinking I had never known such a quiet babe. You've grown into such a beauty, Magen. Just as I knew you would."

"So you're heading back to the farm he left in Vermont?" Bram asked in his big voice. "Our cabin is the first one travelers meet in our small settlement, but still—you winding up in the same dooryard as your folks did all those years ago just based on that tiny little map…I guess mother's right, the angels or someone has guided you to our door."

Magen nodded, at a loss for words.

"So the Creed family still lives there in Vermont?"

"Of that I don't know," Magen said.

"I remember your Pa was bound and determined to move west. Although neither Bram nor I understood why," Sophia said, shaking her head recalling it.

"We tried to get him to stay here in the settlement for a while," Bram said. "But he had gotten it into his head that he must continue the journey he and his bride had started. We couldn't talk him out of it."

"He never did make it to the west," Magen explained. "He stopped in Brooklynne, and there he met Sara, my stepmother. They went to Canada for a while, but that didn't work out. Then they ended up in Sackitt's Ridge where Pa worked a farm and hoped to one day save enough to buy his own." Magen ached for her Pa as she retold his story. "I think traveling alone with a baby was too much for him," Magen said. "That's why he didn't get any further west—because of me."

"I'm sure Sara was just 'the one,' child. You needed a mother and he needed a wife," Sophia surmised, wrapping the past up in a neat-fitting package. "Get some of this in you," she said, and passed a large mug of steaming liquid on a tray. Magen had never tasted anything so delicious or nourishing. "I'll take you down to see where your mother rests in a bit. It's a favorite place of mine," Sophia said quietly, exchanging a look with her husband.

They finished their soup and the three new acquaintances set off down the dusty road. Bram Able was heading back to his forge, and said that he would report Sara's death to the local squire after Magen wrote out all the particulars for him. Sophia and Magen walked with him as far as the cemetery. It was a short walk from the cabin, with a majestic rock cliff as a backdrop.

The cemetery was tucked back in a clearing set off by an intricate wrought-iron fence that must have been made by Able himself. Inside the ring of the fence were three small plain headstones with dates carved in tiny block letters. One larger headstone displayed the family name of Able. Sophia pointed to a stone situated to the left of these. Magen knelt down next to it and ran her fingers over the lettering: Ruth, wife of Samuel Creed, 1781-1798.

"I was not yet a year old," Magen whispered. And then, even more astonished, "She was the age I am now when she died."

"Your Pa sent us enough in coin to pay for the headstone, about a year after he had passed through. It came with a little note that said 'For Ruth's grave, born 1781 died 1798'—nothing more. We weren't sure from where it had been sent, and he didn't say where he had settled. Those two youngn's never got a chance for a life together, did they? Such love between them, too," Sophia said with a shake of the head. "Such a shame you and your Ma never had a chance to get to know one another, Magen. A mother's worst fear, it is. How many of us mind the fact that *right now* is all we can ever count on?"

Magen looked over at the other stone markers, "These are all etched with the name of Able."

"Yes, Bram and I were married right after he got back from fighting Burgoyne in the war. Our children followed right along after that. But as you can see, I only got to keep some of them for a little while." She knelt down to pull a weed from next to one of the stones. "We lost our first born, David. Poor little thing, had no fight in him at all. Our second born, Abraham, Jr., was a bit more fortunate. He's a scrapper and works at his father's side down at the forge. He has a wife and a young son of his own named Zeke, after his great grandfather.

"Then we buried my two young daughters here," Sophia said, placing her worn hands on the one shared headstone. "Twins they were, but three years old. I think God saw how beautiful they were and wanted them back. Golden blonde curls, and bright blue eyes. They got the small pox. They went so fast—within two days of one another. I thought I would die when they went. I wanted to. But I didn't," Sophia said in a voice as quiet as a whisper. "The wonder is we don't die. Too much work to do, I guess."

Forcing a smile and a change of subject, Sophia said, "There aren't that many of us here in the settlement, but one day we'll make a town. You'll see."

"Perhaps … since my mother is buried here. " Magen began. "Perhaps there was a reason my father's map brought me here. Maybe this is where I'm meant to stay. Maybe *this* is where I belong."

Sophia took a while to respond, but then with the utmost kindness she took Magen's hand in both of hers, "Your mother is of another world now, Magen—like my girls. A world we have to let go of while we're in this one. Besides, that map of yours doesn't stop here, does it?"

"But, what if I can't find the Creed family, or perhaps they won't want a stranger—" Magen suddenly felt herself unable to bear the thought of leaving this loving woman or the place where all she knew of her mother remained. Sophia took her by the arm and led her out of the cemetery.

"If by some chance you're unable to find a place for yourself in Vermont, Magen—of course you must return here. You will be welcomed. But family ties abide, child. And I believe you'll find your way."

Chapter 8
The Lake

The Ables insisted that Magen stay the night at their cabin. By the next morning, the dawn broke sunny with a soft breeze blowing from the east.

"You must be feeling anxious about leaving what you know and going into strange territory, Magen. We wouldn't be saying goodbye to you if we didn't believe in our hearts that it's what's best for you," Sophia said as she helped Magen pack up her few belongings.

"Aye, it's your own people you should be with, child. If there are no Creeds left there in Vermont, you come right back to us. You have your mother's beauty and your father's courage. As the wife says, you'll always be welcome here." With that, Magen felt safe; the stopover at the Able's place had made her feel strong and brave again.

After she filled up on cornbread and a mug of tea, Bram and Sophia helped her with Pinetop's riggings. In his loud voice, Bram asked again, "Are ya sure you won't let me escort you at least to the ferry crossing, young Magen?"

Magen shook her head "no"; she was afraid of losing her newfound courage.

"Alright then, girl. Remember, it's less than a day's journey to Rouse's Point where you will find passage across the lake to Vermont."

Magen smiled and assured him she would be all right. Standing on tiptoe, she planted a small kiss on the big man's ruddy cheek. Delighted by this, he said, "Perhaps our paths will cross another day, young Magen." Then he reached out and squeezed her shoulder.

"I pray you have enough joy in your life to balance the sorrows," Sophia whispered to Magen as the two hugged each other goodbye. Magen climbed aboard the wagon reluctantly, tears in her eyes. As she and Pinetop ambled down the road, Magen looked back at the elderly couple and waved. They had inherited the history of each other and were calm with the certainty of it. Magen had always hungered for just such a connection with another and wondered at the possibility of it ever happening to her.

She urged Pinetop on and reflected on what a gift of chance it was to have found this place at all. A gift from her father, she realized, and patted her pocket to ensure that his map was still there.

The sun beat down on her back and Pinetop's. Thinking about what lay ahead, Magen wondered what the lake ferries might look like. She recalled her father telling her how flat boats were used to ferry people and horses across Lake Champlain. But try as she might, she couldn't get a clear picture of something like that in her mind. It must be true, she thought. *How else would she and Pinetop get there?* Staying her course was easier now, at least. The road was well-traveled, in better condition, and in a more accommodating terrain.

Even in the late summer heat, Magen could imagine the slight nip in the air that would come all too soon, and it filled her with a quiet determination to find a place to call home before the snow fell in a few months. She wondered if wanting a thing to happen so hard it made your chest ache was the same as praying; if so, she had done more praying since she left Sackitt's Ridge than she had done in all her seventeen years.

Less than an hour later, just as they wended their way through a rocky cragged hollow, Magen caught sight of a twinkling off in the distance.

"It's the lake, Pinetop!" she said, pointing through the trees. "We'll be there before sunset," she assured the horse and gave his reins a snap.

The air began to smell different. Pinetop seemed to notice it, too, and his measured pace quickened into a canter. At the opening of the road ahead they began to spot cabins with smoke coming from their chimneys. Riders and wagons began to appear on the road around them. The rippling of water reflected the sunlight as the breeze danced across the lake. Magen could hear what she thought must be the sound of waves.

As she approached a wagon that had pulled over and stopped, Magen felt emboldened by the look of two young children who sat watching their father inspect their horse's hoof. Without thinking about it she pulled off her hat to let her hair fall to her back.

"Good day, sir. I hope your horse isn't lame?" she asked, and she flashed a smile at the children.

The man looked up at her and registered mild surprise at seeing an attractive young lady at the reins. He stood up from his crouched position and sized Magen up.

"Just a stone in her foot. I'll soon put her right. Heading across the lake are you?"

"Yes. I need to get over to Vermont," Magen said. "Can you tell me the best way of doing this, sir?"

"I see you don't hail from these parts. Along the shoreline there," he motioned with his hand, "there's always an out-of-work naval boatman or two looking to earn some coin."

"I see," Magen replied. "I come from Sackitt's Ridge, a few days west of here. My family awaits me in Vermont." She had added on this information for no particular reason except that it felt good to be conversing with a passing stranger.

"Where in Vermont is your family?" the man asked. His two young boys sat looking at Magen with interest.

"My family's farm is in a place called Saint Rock. It shows here on my map. Do you know of it?" Magen pulled the map out of her pocket.

"Ah, yes. The village near Tucker Gorge, t'other side of Fat Mountain," the man said.

"Other side?" Magen questioned, inspecting again the faded markings on the cloth map—which in no way indicated a mountain on either side of Saint Rock.

"Not exactly a fat mountain, as mountains go," the man drawled. "It's more like a large hill." The two boys grinned at their father's wit.

Magen thanked the man and urged Pinetop on. She reached the shoreline less than a quarter of an hour later. She was excited now and wanted to see more of the lake. She pulled the wagon over and tied Pinetop off.

Magen decided to hide her hair again so as not to draw attention. Small groups of militia units could be seen marching in the distance, or milling in small groups here and there. People took little notice of her, nor did she spot anyone that looked like they were in the business of ferrying. After a few minutes more of walking in the hot afternoon sun, Magen pulled her cap off again and rubbed the sweat off of her neck with it. She came upon a bateau moored at a small dock in the cove. Cupping her hand to her mouth she hailed the man she could see unloading it.

"Do you ferry people across the lake?" Magen yelled to him.

He stood up straight and turned to look at her. "That I do, Miss."

Chapter 9

Gabriel and the Ferry

The man was not much older than herself. Magen would normally have been too shy to approach if she had been able to ascertain his age from a distance—it didn't seem proper somehow, and now she was embarrassed. He stood smiling at her and brazenly looked her up and down.

"And where is your mother, young lady?" he asked. "That is, you are a young lady and not a young man. Correct?"

"I have seventeen years to my credit. I'm not a child," Magen said, suddenly feeling defensive. "I've had a long journey, mostly by foot. That's why I'm dressed this way."

"My apologies. I can see you're not a child," Gabriel smiled. Magen was unsure how she should reply to that, so she changed the subject.

"I must reach the other side of the lake. I have family in Vermont outside of Saint Rock. Although on closer examination it appears questionable whether your boat can ferry both me and my horse to the other side."

"There are larger boats just north and south, if you have time and money. But I assure you this vessel is adequate and it's a calm enough day on the lake. If you think you can handle it, I'll be returning to the other side as soon as I have unloaded this last bit of cargo."

Magen was dubious and didn't respond.

"Miss, the village of Saint Rock is over Fat Mountain. I'll be heading into Windmill Point at Alburgh—a good starting point for your destination. I can take you and your horse across for a small fee. You'll have to leave the wagon for another time though. My name is Gabriel Thayer, by the way. And whom do I have the honor of addressing?"

"My name is Magen Creed. You seem quite young to be captain of your own boat," she said. She was stalling as she tried to check out the stability and seaworthiness of the gaff-rigged wooden vessel.

Noting her hesitancy and nervousness, Gabe offered her his hand and then pulled her onboard before she could change her mind. With a big smile he said, "I assure you I am old enough to captain this vessel, Miss Creed, just as I am sure that you are old enough to be my passenger. Seventeen is a ripe fair age and you look as though you've seen some adventure. I find it hard to believe your family allowed you to travel alone, though."

"I buried what was left of my family along the way," Magen said in a quiet voice.

He looked surprised. "I'm sorry, miss," he said, and sounded as though he meant it. "In fact, this boat belongs to a friend of mine. He's not been well and needed someone to take over his ferrying and deliveries for a bit. This happens to be my last run. I am a carpenter, you see. I build homes and barns and all manner of buildings," Gabriel said, with such pride Magen had to smile.

"But I'm humble enough to take on other work when I must. Shall I go and get your horse then, Magen, or would you feel safer on a larger boat?"

"I'll come with you! To get Pinetop, I mean," Magen said; she did not want to be left on the boat alone.

"Of course, he'll be less skittish if you bring him aboard."

Aware that the young captain-carpenter was casting interested sidelong glances at her as they walked back up the shoreline, Magen also tried discreetly to inspect him. He was quick to smile, and he certainly knew how to be charming. There was something about him that made him seem trustworthy enough, *or did she find him trustworthy because she found him handsome?* Tall and dark haired, he had an easy way about him that reminded Magen of her father. When she tried to meet his gaze though, she found herself suddenly shy and looked away.

Gabriel started to joke about the long-standing feuds between the "Yorkers" and Vermonters, and Magen broke in suddenly: "We lived in Sackitt's Ridge. But there was an accident, you see, along the way. My stepmother got caught under the wheel of the wagon and died. I buried her on the trail just four days ago."

Embarrassed that she had blurted such a thing out with no warning, Magen wondered why she had shared that. Now having Sara's death hang in the air between them felt awkward. She turned away from him, her face burning.

Gabriel came to a full stop. He reached out and put a hand on her shoulder. Magen forced herself to turn and look at him and was surprised by the look of concern on his face.

"So you are on your own, then?" he asked.

"I am," she said, aware that this man had an intensity about him that was different than the schoolboys back in Sackitt's Ridge. She had to first think through what she wanted to say next and hoped this didn't make her appear slow or dimwitted. "I am looking for the family Creed's homestead. According to my map it's not far. I thought perhaps it was located this side of the Mountain." She showed him the map from her pocket. "But a man I met earlier said that the village the farm is located near is on the other side."

"You mean the village of Saint Rock," he said looking at her map. "You said your name is Creed? Is it the Female Farmer's place you are looking for then?"

"The Female Farmer?" Magen asked.

"I don't know her Christian name. But her surname is Creed, and she's known around these parts as the 'Female Farmer.' There aren't many women in the area who manage their own homestead as she does. Take no offense, but you look as though you could be her relation." He smiled and he gestured toward her manner of dress. Magen giggled as she looked down at her ragged appearance.

"I haven't met Miss Creed," Gabriel said, "but I am acquainted with her hired man. He has recommended me for carpentry work in the past. Her farm is inland. South of Windmill Point where we will land, and then over the Notch. It's true it's on the other side of Fat Mountain, but not to worry—the mountain's not so fat," he said, as the other man had said, and then he too smiled at his own cleverness.

"So I've been told," Magen said, rolling her eyes.

"My own family hails from Bellingham. It's a bit further east from Saint Rock. So you see, you happened along at just the right bend in the lake, miss. You found a waterman who happens to be going your way. Knowing who you're related to goes some way in explaining how you could manage such a dangerous journey on your own. Independence must run in the family."

"If there had been a choice in the matter, I would not have faced the journey alone, Mr. Thayer."

"Most people call me Gabriel or Gabe. May I call you Mae?"

"My name is Magen."

"Mae suits you better," he said, without a hint of mocking.

Magen felt a pang. Her father was the only one who ever called her Mae before.

"Many of the big farms are well known in the area," Gabe continued. "If only by name. Creed Farm is not that big, but it is known for its quality herd. The Creed name has been known in these parts for as long as I can remember. There was a brother or something, wasn't there?" he asked.

"You must mean my father. He left the farm just before I was born. You say it is the sister then who runs the place now, on her own? My grandparents must be dead then. I never met them. She doesn't know I'm coming."

"From what I know of her, she keeps to herself," Gabriel continued. "I didn't know there were Creeds across the lake in New York. You will be welcomed enough here I should think. As long as you don't broadcast the fact that you are a 'Yorker.'"

Magen was about to protest until she saw the grin on his face and the twinkle in his eye.

Chapter 10

An Overnight

The two of them managed to get a nervous Pinetop over the wooden ramp and onto the thirty-foot boat. It was a simple craft with a worn-looking sail and an upturned end on the starboard side. Gabriel pushed off from the shore with a long-poled hook.

"We'll not be crossing at the broad side of the lake, miss. It will take us less than an hour to get there."

Feeling as unsettled as Pinetop, Magen tried to hide the fact that this was the first time she had ever been on a boat. Although she and Carrie had joined the other schoolchildren playing in the shallow water of the creek behind the schoolhouse, she could not swim, and her fear of going overboard was beginning to make her nauseous. Trying to look composed, she braced herself for the ride as Gabriel took hold of the wheel.

With assistance from a warm breeze, they made it a good way from shore before much time had passed. Gabriel smiled at Magen; she was white-knuckling Pinetop's lead rope.

"If the water makes you nervous, you can sit a spell," Gabe called out. "Your horse appears to be enjoying it now. I'll tell you when we're about to reach the other side."

Pinetop had settled in and did look to be enjoying the ride. Magen dropped down onto the small wooden bench and exhaled. She willed herself to relax and try to enjoy the unusual experience of floating on such a huge body of water. She spotted other sailing vessels farther out and going in both directions. They came in all shapes and sizes—some carrying cargo, others carrying passengers. Magen liked the rhythmic slap of the water on the side of the boat and savored the feel of the last of the afternoon sun warming her face. Pinetop made low nickering sounds as the breeze cooled him off.

Magen stole a look up at Gabriel as he managed the helm. He wore his dark wavy hair long, pulled back in a leather tie. He had dark green eyes that seemed to take everything in at once, and he had an intelligent smile with good teeth. He was tall and slender; he had a square jaw and a crease between his brows. Even though Magen was certain Gabe wasn't much older than herself, he carried himself as though he had some experience. Her anxiety and tension began to melt away. She rested her head on Pinetop's smooth warm neck and began to doze. The next thing she realized, Gabriel nudged her awake. The sail came down and they arrived at Windmill Point.

Gabriel hailed a man on the shore who grabbed the rope hoisted to him. Gabe then used the long pole to maneuver the boat alongside the shoreline. He pulled the boat into the dock that awaited them and dropped the side gate of the boat. It acted as a ramp to the shore. Gabe pulled Pinetop off by his lead rope, and Magen followed behind. Gabe smiled broadly and made a grand gesture with his hand, "Go and explore, young Magen. A brand new place welcomes you!"

There were a few buildings off of the piers and along the main road of the small but bustling lake village. People were walking in all directions along the dirt road going about their errands. Magen heard a Frenchman converse with a woman carrying a market basket in one arm and a baby in her other. She watched the woman, impressed with the confident way in which she dealt with both the Frenchman and the baby. The sounds of a boy on the corner hawking newspapers competed with the fishwife calling out her catch of the day. Carts of fruits and vegetables stood outside storefronts as horses and people passed one another eyeing the merchandise. Magen was self-conscious of her attire when she saw how colorfully-dressed some of the women were. But it was all so new to her she soon forgot about what she was wearing.

She turned back to Gabe, who was finishing his business with the man who met the boat. He smiled at her and nodded toward the clock tower of the Meeting House. "It occurs to me that you might like to stay overnight at the local inn," he said. "I happen to know the proprietor of the Inn, and would see that you are given safe lodging at a fair price. I'll sleep on the boat, of course. And in the morning I will personally escort you to the Creed homestead."

Magen turned all of this over in her head. She knew that she owed for the ferry service, and she didn't like the idea of spending what little she had so early in her journey. In addition to that anxiety, she was unsure if she had the currency that they used here. Magen took a leap of faith and showed Gabriel her collection of coins.

"Ah," he said. "This one will take care of a bed for you and food, as well as the ferry passage."

By Magen's calculations she had gotten a good deal. Relieved, she smiled at Gabe. "I confess, the thought of meeting my aunt for the first time after this long, amazing day was more than I could face. Thank you."

Gabriel smiled at her and gestured the way to the inn as he took Pinetop's reins. The inn also housed the town tavern. There they spoke to the proprietor who instructed his wife to take Magen in hand. "Another woman's traveling to visit her elderly mother—you'll room with her," the innkeeper said.

Gabriel handed Magen her haversack and called to her back, "I hope you sleep soundly, Mae Creed. I'll take care that your horse is fed and bedded down proper, and I will see you in the morning."

Magen felt a rush of gratitude and waved. She followed the talkative matron up the stairs, a betty lamp lighting their way.

As exhausted as Magen was, she marveled at the experience of staying at an inn that one paid coin for! The woman showed her a bowl and pitcher of water in the little alcove just off of her room, and gave her clean linen to wash up with. Magen scrubbed herself as best she could and hoped Pinetop was getting a good brush down as well. When she opened the door to her room, she found her roommate already asleep in the bed; it appeared barely large enough for one more occupant. Magen spotted the chamber pot at the foot of the bed and hoped she would not have need of it. She took off her britches, but left on her underclothes. She gently slid into bed next to the snoring woman. *How odd to sleep with a total stranger,* Magen thought just before nodding off to sleep.

The next morning she brushed out her long hair and donned the simple cotton trousers and vest she had in her haversack, all the while wondering at what the day would bring. Her roommate, already up and dressed, was a woman of perhaps thirty who chattered on about making the last leg of her journey to visit her mother in southern Vermont. Magen listened attentively to the woman but evaded her questions when she inquired as to Magen's situation. It was too complicated a story to try and explain in passing, so Magen simply said she was returning home to Saint Rock.

The two women said their goodbyes, and Magen made her way downstairs with haversack in hand. Within minutes she was sitting in a sunny window seat in the dining hall, drinking tea from a steaming mug when Gabriel sauntered in and smiled down at her.

"Sipping tea like the Queen," he said in a teasing manner. "I trust you slept well last night?"

Surprised at the delight she felt at seeing him, she replied that she had. He sat down at the table across from her as she continued: "I was thinking what a shame my father never brought us here to visit his only sister. I know so little about his life before he married my stepmother. I'm afraid my aunt is in for quite a shock—finding out she has a niece who has no home."

"I don't pretend to understand the ways of family," Gabriel said, helping himself to a mug from a side cabinet. "Certainly not my family, anyway. But I would be thinking that your aunt would be grateful for an extra set of hands and some family with whom to share the farm. It can't have been easy for her, living alone. We'll learn soon enough how you'll fare."

"Mr. Thayer, there is no need for you to deliver me to her door. I've made it this far alone. I can manage on my own if you have business elsewhere."

"My ferrying duties have come to an end, and after what you have been through, Miss Creed, I could not allow you to finish the journey alone. Besides, it's far from an inconvenience for me. Your aunt's hired hand, Mr. Mackay, may have word of carpentry work for hire."

Magen was a little disappointed that she wasn't the sole reason for his decision to accompany her, but she didn't let on. "Will you be going on to your family's home in Bellingham afterward?"

"Perhaps. But my apprenticeship days are over. I go wherever the work is now. I'll see how Tucker Gorge and Saint Rock are placed for carpenters… besides," he said, hesitating a little, "I would really like to see you safely delivered to your new home."

"I am obliged," she grinned.

Chapter 11

Over the Notch

After packing up her few belongings from the room, Magen met Gabriel out in front of the Inn. He had retrieved Pinetop, who looked as though he too had benefited from a good night's sleep. Gabe was mounted on a powerful-looking black horse Magen had never seen the likes of before.

"A schoolmaster named Morgan acquired this breed from a man in Massachusetts and brought him home to his farm in Randolph. They're marvelous horses to ride and good workers. Since no one's quite sure of their true bloodlines, they call them Morgans. I was fortunate enough to be owed a sum for work I completed—short of currency, the man chose to pay me with Toby here. I've never been happier with a deal's outcome."

"I'm sure Toby and Pinetop will be great friends," Magen said, and they rode out in high spirits.

Magen didn't remember ever being anywhere but Sackitt's Ridge and wished she could have seen more of Windmill Point, but she was nonetheless delighted to be back on horseback, riding with Gabriel, on so beautiful a day. It took a couple of hours of invigorating riding up hills and down to climb over the notch of Fat Mountain.

Lush, and filled with the flora and fauna of late summer, the deep green landscape was set off by a hundred other colors Magen tried to take in—the luscious reds of the staghorn sumac, the last of the wild blue phlox and the purple milkweed—so much beauty, Magen thought. It almost hurt to look at it all.

Gabriel knew the landscape and was a good guide. "Over that rise of giant hemlock is a lumber mill. The miller who lives there has a family of twelve children," he explained. A little further along, he told Magen that the local tribe of Abenaki Indians who wintered in the area call Lake Champlain "Petonbowk."

"It means the 'waters that lie between' the Adirondacks and our beautiful Green Mountains."

Magen knew Gabriel was trying to impress her with his knowledge, and she saw no need to point out to him that the landscape on the New York side of the lake looked more impressive than that of the Vermont side. He obviously was proud of his Vermont home, and she enjoyed listening to him. Although she could not explain it to herself, Magen had felt all morning as if she were coming home. She wanted to savor the journey a while longer. "Could we stop awhile? Perhaps get a drink from the stream?" she asked.

She could see Gabriel liked the idea. He dismounted his horse first, then offered his arms to help her dismount. Magen felt butterflies in her stomach, reached for his shoulders, and was delighted at how natural she felt within his grasp. When he realized he was holding on to her just the slightest bit too long they both smiled, and he set her down.

"After you have delivered me to my aunt's, will we ever see each other again?" Her boldness surprised her, but Magen did not regret asking the question. He looked at her like he was trying to remember her from another time and place.

"Oh, we'll see each other," was all he said, but somehow it was enough.

After they helped themselves to a drink from the cold mountain stream they stood back and let the horses quench their thirst.

"Do you come from a long line of carpenters?" she asked.

"Hardly," Gabriel said, as he got comfortable on one of the huge rocks that lined the banks. "My father fought at the Battle of Valcour in '76. He was but eighteen and full of the devil and pride. A musket ball tore into his spine and left him a cripple. He reclaimed some of his strength. But he's been unfit for a normal day's work from that day to this."

Seeing Magen's uneasiness, he added "Being an educated man, my Pa has never been idle. He has spent his many years since that war tutoring and teaching the ignorant young minds of Bellingham."

"And did you assist him in his teaching?" Magen asked.

"My father knew me well enough to know that I did not have the calling of a teacher. He sent me away when I was twelve to apprentice with Ira Saint Amand for seven years. Saint Amand was one of the best finish carpenters in all of Vermont. I learned a lot from him and I enjoyed my journeyman days. But now I'm beholden to no man. Saint Amand, now a captain in the Vermont militia, had me serve guard duty along the border in this last fiasco with the British."

"Not so popular a cause, this engagement," Magen said.

Shaking his head in disgust, Gabriel continued. "Here we were, farmers to a man, expected to protect the border from British invasion, and yet we were given no arms to speak of. Many had only the guns they used in the last war, or none at all! I was fortunate in the end, Saint Amand later enlisted my services as a shipbuilder. I had more need of a hammer than a gun, and I was glad of it. Like others, I was not so keen to fight for policies that made paupers out of so many here in the north."

"Your family must be glad that you didn't have to go to battle," Magen said.

"My father has become a peace-loving man over the years. He is as loved by his students as he is harassed by his wife," he paused. "My mother, you see, thought she was marrying an up-and-coming young officer in one of Boston's finest military families. She was sure his career would take them both to great heights within the best social circles. Alas, she has had to rely on her own family's modest wealth to keep her and my sister living on at least the perimeter of high society."

Magen wasn't sure how to respond. "Did your father teach you before you became an apprentice?" she asked.

"Yes, and Saint Amand insisted that I continue the book learning I began when I was young. In fact, my father made it part of the bargain. So I can read and write, but I'm more at home with my chisels and hammer than with a book."

"This country needs carpenters as well as scholars," Magen said— thinking that her own father would have liked and agreed with Gabriel's sentiments.

Gabriel shifted his shoulders against the rock he leaned on. "Yes. Having taken on the Brits twice now, we Americans have showed them we are equal to both kings and queens," he said, echoing the popular sentiment in the North.

"You have strong convictions, Mr. Thayer."

"If you will stop calling me that, I promise to stop pontificating. I'm just Gabe." His smile then would have made her swoon if she was of that inclination.

Magen liked hearing him talk and would have stretched the conversation out a bit longer, but Gabe said, "I'm sure you're anxious to meet your aunt now and stop sitting here listening to me talk on. I forget myself."

"I guess perhaps it is time we were off," Magen said reluctantly. *What if her aunt didn't want anything to do with her?* Magen pushed the unbidden thought away. Gabriel had noticed the look of anxiety that briefly appeared on her face.

"Are you worried, Magen? Your eyes give you away sometimes. They're quite expressive."

Magen felt herself blush, and she gave him a grateful nod. Rarely had she had anyone pay such close attention to her. "Just wondering how my aunt will react to discovering family she knew nothing of."

"I think if she does not welcome you, Mae, she is not the unique person people credit her for being."

They rode for perhaps an hour more along a winding dirt path coming down from Fat Mountain. Just as they rounded a bend, the horses became agitated. Gabriel pulled back on Toby's reins with a look of alarm on his face. "Can you smell that smoke? That's coming from the direction of Creed Farm."

They took off again at a full gallop. As they rounded the last curve they got a clear view of a barn—or what was left of a large gable-ended structure. They both dismounted in a rush and looked out at the sorry site of the collapsed building. The fire was so recent that all that was left was a shattered field of smoking embers. The two young travelers stood stunned, and as the coals crackled Gabe put his arm around Magen's shoulders.

Chapter 12
Aunt Eliza

"Did you already hear there would be work for a carpenter, lad?" a gravelly voice called out from behind them. Magen and Gabriel turned to see a tall, gaunt, gray-haired man walking toward them. His bristled face had deep lines etched around the mouth and eyes; Magen liked him on sight for the patience she saw in his eyes. He was covered in soot and looked exhausted, but he stood calmly with an air of endurance about him.

"What's happened here, Mr. Mackay?" Gabriel asked.

"We were up with a sick ewe 'til all hours," the man started to explain in a raspy Scottish accent. "Both so tired we couldn't see straight, Eliza and I. The lantern got knocked over, and, well, with the dry weather things went up in a matter of minutes."

"You mean, *I* knocked over the lantern, Avery. Don't you go taking the blame for my clumsiness," said a husky voice behind Avery. "Seeing the smoke, our good neighbors came running. But it was too late. We just had time to form a chain from the well." Eliza Creed was dressed in leather breeches and covered with soot. She spoke in a deep hoarse voice. "It's been so dry. We're just fortunate the wind wasn't up."

"With Louise and George Reynolds' help, we kept it from reaching the other buildings, and we managed to save the animals. That's all that matters. Barns can be rebuilt—can they not, Master Thayer?" Avery said cocking an eye toward Gabriel.

"Thayer, is it?" Eliza looked over at Gabriel now. "You've done some work at the Reynolds place before, I think."

"Yes, ma'm. And I know you from your reputation, Miss Creed," Gabriel said a little nervously.

"Yes. I can just imagine what that might be," Eliza smiled. "Well, it must be providence that sent a carpenter to us first thing this morning," she said, trying to smile past a cloud of smoke that billowed from a sooty pile of refuse.

"Bring your friend on up to the house," Eliza pointed to Magen. "I need to make up a poultice for Avery's hand. And a jug of switchel might just slake my thirst."

Gabriel looked at Magen, shrugged his shoulders, and began to follow Eliza toward the farmhouse. Soon they were all trudging in line behind Eliza Creed to the house on the hill.

It was a typical New England saltbox—a pine clapboard fortress against the brutal Vermont winters. Its gabled ends set east and west. The kitchen and main living area were heated by the southern exposure in the front, and the back parlor and bedrooms were protected from the north winds with a sloping hand-rived shingle roof. The main chimney stood in the middle of the roof like a centerpiece.

Surrounded on the hill by giant oak and butternut trees, the house's dooryard contained two sugar maples—husband-and-wife trees, Magen suspected, planted as a tribute to a couple who lived here long ago. The view of the surrounding farm from the dooryard gate made Magen's heart sing.

Creed Farm looked like a rich man's farm compared to the small scruff of land her father had worked in Sackitt's Ridge. It had a number of out-buildings and one other large barn next to the one that had burned. The farm's rolling hills were dotted with fat white herds of sheep. Magen could hear them bleating in the distance. Entering the stump fence of the dooryard, Magen noticed herbs and flowers planted all along the perimeter of the house. She recognized many that Sara had tried to grow for her kitchen and medicine cabinet.

As they walked into the kitchen, they were greeted by a crackling fire in the cavernous stone hearth. A giant wooden spinner took up much of the south corner of the room. Eliza dropped her soot-covered hat onto the walnut trestle table situated in the center of the room next to the fire. Dressed in a man's clothing similar to what Magen herself had on, Eliza's britches and boots were covered with ash and dirt. Magen couldn't quite make out her features through the grime on her face, but she noticed her eyes. Eliza's eyes were hazel with deep laugh lines on either side; they sparkled with curiosity. Immediately seeing the resemblance to her father, Magen had to remind herself to breathe. Magen watched Eliza hurry around gathering jars of powders and packets of roots from the wooden cupboard.

"Pulverized ginger and slippery elm made into a poultice will help his arm, I should think," Eliza muttered more to herself than to anyone in the room. Just as she turned with jar in hand, she stopped short. Eliza Creed seemed to take the measure of first Gabriel and then Magen. Staring at her, unembarrassed and in no hurry, she said in a soft but controlled voice: "Who are you, child?"

Magen felt so foolish all of a sudden—hoping to try and explain herself and her situation to this woman who had just lost her barn to a fire. She wished she could somehow disappear through the cracks in the wide-planked floor.

"I'm...my name is Magen...Magen Creed, Aunt. I am your brother Samuel's daughter."

Eliza Creed stood frozen, without saying a word. Magen scrambled to think of what else she could say.

"I've come to find you, as you are the only family I have left now. I'm sorry I have picked such an unfortunate moment to arrive." With that she stopped. She could see her aunt was stunned. She didn't want to make it worse by chattering like a magpie.

Eliza grabbed hold of the end of the table for support. Magen saw the color drain away from her aunt's soot-covered face, and became afraid that Eliza might faint. Mr. Mackay stood mute as well. Magen looked over at Gabriel and got no comfort there, either. "I'll go to the spring and get you some water, shall I, Aunt?"

"No, child. Thank you. Avery, I'll take some of the hard cider. One of the jugs from out back in the buttery, if you don't mind."

Avery left the room and returned with a large stone jug. He poured some cider into a tin cup and handed it to Eliza, who stood looking at Magen still.

"Tell me your name again, girl."

"Magen, ma'am."

"Our mother's maiden name …" Eliza said, gesturing toward a shelf that held a few small painted likenesses of men and women whom Magen assumed to be family members.

"Lavinia Magen. The Magen family hailed from Boston. But I guess you've been told all this."

"No. I haven't. I always assumed Magen had been a name from my mother's side. Pa never told me much—about his family, that is." Magen stumbled along self-consciously. *Why had she never asked her Pa how she got her name?*

"My brother was never a great one for talk. He wrote once to tell me that Ruth had gotten sick and died, but that you were all right. That was the only and last time I heard from him. He never made it west then," Eliza said as if pondering aloud. After a moment she looked up at Magen, "You say you're alone, child?"

"We lived in Sackitt's Ridge. Pa wanted to earn enough to get out of New York, so he took up smuggling. He ran a herd of horses across the border in 1813. Sara and I—she being the woman Pa married after Ma died—heard later he got caught up in a skirmish and may have gotten killed. We don't know for certain. We've never received official word one way or another.

"Sara and I left Sackitt's Ridge after my half-sister Carrie died of the Genessee fever. We wouldn't have survived there another winter just the two of us. So I thought it was time to try and find Pa's family. He left this map, you see ... Anyway, Sara, she got pinned under the wagon wheel on our way here. She died, Aunt Eliza. Along the trail there. I buried her myself."

"My word," Eliza looked awed.

Telling her story out loud, Magen heard how pitiful it all sounded and did not want these people to feel sorry for her. She decided to save the tale of the Ables and her Ma's grave for another time.

"We fully intended on working for our keep, Aunt. If you have work for me to do, that is. If you would care to take on another mouth to feed, I'd be obliged, as that is the arrangement Sara and I had hoped for. If it isn't convenient for you, say so—please. I can read, and the schoolmaster taught me to write and do some cyphering. I am suited to most kinds of work, I think. At least I'm willing. I could return to the village and seek employment there if you have no need of me here."

"Whoa, child. Let me catch my breath a minute. You must be about seventeen by now? Seeing you standing in front of me, with that clear look of Creed in your face, kind of makes a thing like a burned barn seem unimportant," Eliza said with a faint smile, allowing Magen to breathe once more. Eliza then walked over to her neice and took her by the shoulders. Looking straight into Magen's face, she smiled. And this time it reached her eyes. The ice broke. The tension lifted.

"I would say we are all entitled to a drink of cider," Eliza said. "Avery, you don't mind, do you?"

"I'll be happy to oblige," he said.

As everyone but Avery stood drinking a bit of potent cider, Eliza put her arm around Magen's shoulder. "I'm not used to family, as you can see, Magen. Please come and sit down. Let's all sit a moment and catch our breath."

"I should be going, then," Gabriel said.

"You can sit a moment, too, Mr. Thayer. You'll not drop off my long-lost niece and then turn around and leave."

"No, ma'am. I mean, of course, I'll stay," he stammered.

"You sure do have the look of a Creed," Avery said to Magen.

"She's easily the prettiest of the Creeds," Eliza said.

"Eliza will appreciate the company of another female, I'm sure. A nice break from my poor conversation," Avery said with a grin.

Magen looked at Eliza as they sat across from one another at the table. In her aunt, Magen saw a slightly different version of her father. She had the high cheekbones and the chiseled Creed face. Her black hair was pulled back in a bun, with a few wisps escaping and softly framing her bright, intelligent eyes. Her mouth formed a wide and generous smile. She held herself straight and had a proud bearing.

"Surprises come all at once, now don't they?" Eliza said. "First my barn. And now, well, now it looks as though things are turning around. I've got a family," she said with a quick laugh.

"After Samuel left, the folks—your grandparents—both got sick and died, Magen. Your Pa never knew that, did he?"

"No, Aunt."

"I wanted to write to him," Eliza explained. "He said he would let me know when he found his place. That's the way he put it—'his place.' He never knew he could return to the farm," Eliza's words drifted off into her own thoughts again.

"Pa never talked much about his own father, but I know he always missed this place. Right before he left for Canada he left me this small map. It's the map to Creed Farm."

Eliza's head shook in a kind of despair. "That doesn't surprise me. He left under a dark cloud, as far as our Pa was concerned anyway. That's why I'm farming this place and he's not. He and our Pa never saw eye to eye. There's plenty of room, as you can see. I don't know how I'll do, as family, mind you—I don't know what you're used to. But this is the Creed Farm, and you are a Creed and are most welcome to stay."

Magen looked over at Gabriel, who was smiling now. Her heart felt like it might burst in her chest. To her own and everyone else's surprise, she got up, went around the table, and kissed her aunt on the cheek. She couldn't say anything as her tears began to fall.

Eliza did not react at first, but then her arms encircled Magen and she pulled her in close. She didn't speak either, but her embrace was strong and warm. Magen had never known such comfort.

Chapter 13
The Saltbox House

With very few words, much had been settled that first day, Magen reminisced as she filled the iron kettle with water from the pipe in the pantry for morning tea. She had been at Creed Farm more than a fortnight now, and she loved the place a little more every day. The kitchen was the most lived-in room of the house. The long walnut trestle table that always smelled of beeswax occupied a good part of the sunny room.

Eliza's front parlor had a few pieces that had belonged to Magen's grandmother, and the Magen family coat-of-arms hung next to the Creed coat-of-arms over the mantle. In the winter months this room would be closed off altogether to conserve heat.

Eliza slept just off the kitchen on the first floor, close to the hearth. Magen slept in the room at the top of the stairs. Just down the hallway was an alcove where two young sisters from a neighboring family—Jane and Emmy—slept when they were working for Eliza. Jane and Emmy were twelve and ten years old respectively and came from a large local family with more mouths to feed than they could provide for. A similar arrangement of hired hands applied to the rest of the farm as well. The heavy workloads at harvest and lambing time required extra help, and quite often it was local families down on their luck who loaned out their children or their own services to the more profitable farms to work in exchange for food or crops or food and board.

At first Magen felt bad for their situation, but two more cheerful girls could not be found. They claimed that working at Creed Farm wasn't nearly as difficult as being at home—and the food was more plentiful. With Magen now living at the farm, chores could be divided up more evenly. And ten-year-old Emmy, who was not physically strong, was allowed to do more of the weaving. She enjoyed that more than the outside farmwork.

Jane had been organizing the storage attic above the kitchen this morning while Magen dealt with preparing the soup pot for the field workers. The hallway leading off the kitchen to the back contained the larder, the spring room, and the drying and curing room. Beyond that, there was the privy closet—a luxury to Magen, who had grown up with an outdoor privy shed that obliged one to freeze in winter and bake in summer. Once a week, Magen and Eliza hung blankets from hooks in the kitchen ceiling to surround a tin tub that they strategically placed in front of the hearth in order to take turns having a bath. It was a great deal of extra work, but neither minded; they both looked forward to the weekly ritual.

This morning the fire had already heated the large kitchen up to an uncomfortable temperature. Magen opened the east window for any small breeze, and pushed her hair off of her sweaty face. Looking out toward the field, she saw Gabriel working in the distance. He had been offered the work of helping Mr. Mackay rebuild the barn. Magen was delighted that he had accepted. She had never felt drawn to a man before now, and she couldn't seem to decide if it was terrifying or exciting. *Both*, she thought, smiling to herself as the coolness of the breeze played across her face. Anytime Gabriel was near, Magen's skin tingled with excitement. From the look in his eyes, Magen knew he felt the same way.

Once Eliza and Avery came in from looking after the herds, the rest of the workers were called in for their mid-day meal. Jane teased Magen that she should put on her best smile because "gorgeous Gabe" was on his way to the house. Magen pretended to scold Jane for being insubordinate, but knew that Jane respected her and would never take advantage of her position in Eliza's house. It was her way of being friendly with Magen, and Magen appreciated the camaraderie.

Magen was able to sit across from Gabe when she wasn't dishing out more stew. And even though they couldn't converse in their usual way, it was a treat just to be near each other.

After the meal was finished and everyone got back to their chores, Magen was left on her own in the kitchen. She took the treenware out through the breezeway to the spring room to be washed. She liked it out there where it was cool; it was a great improvement over carrying water in from the creek outside of the cabin in Sackitt's Ridge. At Creed Farm, the greasy dishwater was collected in a barrel and Magen would later pour it over the ash barrel and use it for the soapmaking. It wasn't that there was less work on Creed Farm than at Sackitt's Ridge—there was considerably more. But a certain devotion to the land existed here that Magen never experienced in Sackitt's Ridge. There, the relentless grind of doing-without depleted the human spirit. *What grace had been given to her that she should find this place, and that it should bear the name of Creed?*

Over the last few weeks, Magen and Gabe had gotten into the habit of taking long after-dinner walks together through the fields. As long as Eliza and Avery could see them from the porch where they sat, propriety was felt to be observed.

"Your Aunt Eliza looks on you as though you're the long lost sheep who has found her way home at last. Don't you think, Mae?" Gabe asked. He often used her father's nickname for her now, and Magen felt this tied the three of them together. Although she hadn't told Gabe, she knew her father would have liked him. "I think it's *me* your aunt is a bit unsure of, after all."

"It's just Eliza being careful—watching over me. That's what families do, don't they?" Magen asked. Gabe looked at Magen and realized how much it meant to her to have family that cared.

"Yes, that's exactly what families do, Magen."

Having never had a best friend, Magen, had at first been wary of sharing her personal thoughts with Gabriel. She feared he would think her silly. But it didn't take long to get over that feeling; Gabe seemed to hang on her every word. They laughed at all the same things, and it wasn't long before they were finishing each other's sentences.

"It's like the two are from the same pod," Avery commented, as he pointed his pipe toward the meadow where he and Eliza sat and watched Magen and Gabe walking in the fields. "Can you not see that, Eliza?"

"Who, Avery?"

"The two young ones!" Avery repeated with urgency. Seeing Eliza's skepticism he added, "Ach! There's no doubt about it, woman!"

"They're just children, Mr. Mackay. Least ways, Magen is. Let's just let it alone, shall we? If it's meant to be, then it will be. They don't need our encouragement."

When Eliza referred to him as Mr. Mackay, Avery knew better than to risk a debate.

Chapter 14

Worrying Signs

As Magen went through the dooryard out to the stables one cloudy morning, she spotted something amiss in the south meadow. A small group of frantic sheep had separated from the herd and was running from one end of the field to the other. She could hear their distressed bleating and knew something was wrong. She yelled for Eliza but got no response. Then she yelled in the direction of the barn for Avery or Gabriel, and didn't see anyone. Withought further thought, she ran back inside the house and grabbed the flintlock rifle hanging above the hearth. With trembling hands and a wildly beating heart, she made her way back out to the meadow.

It didn't take long before she spotted a dark creature skulking among the herd, then another. Every Vermonter knew the hazard that wolves could wreak on a herd of sheep. Magen unscrewed the cap of the powder horn with her teeth, spilling some on the ground and tasting the bitter hint of sulfur. Hefting the long weapon up to her shoulder, she tried to keep the slender barrel of the gun steady. It was too big a gamble to rely on her marksmanship, Magen thought, *what if she were to kill one of the herd?*

Instead, she raised the gun straight up and fired. The jolt knocked her backwards and her shoulder throbbed, but she could see the herd scatter. She also spotted one wolf taking off toward the treeline, followed closely by the other. Avery came running up from one of the outbuildings, hammer in hand. Magen handed him the gun, and breathlessly described what she had seen. Avery took off for the meadow, with Gabriel joining him from another direction. Magen waited until they had reached the herd before she went to check on the safety of the barn animals.

There had been three wolves, Avery later explained as they sat around the dinner table. He thought he clipped the last of them in the shoulder with a round of shot, but not before the wolf had brought down one of the young lambs and dragged it off.

"Fortunately, the other two had been scared off by Magen's shot before they got to the panicked ewes," Avery said, with a nod of approval toward Magen. "We were lucky this time. Even a small pack of wolves can wipe out a large herd."

Eliza had been working in the north pasture at the time of the attack and hadn't heard any of the commotion. But she looked the most worried now.

"Attacks in daylight hours—a bad sign," she said, thinking out loud. "Last year's deep snows and low temperatures have left them undernourished and hungry. There've been bounties posted in town, but so far few wolves have been brought in. We'll need to put a couple more shepherds out there with dogs, especially in that field banked by the forest. Too easy for them to attack. Avery, see if the Hart brothers can help us out—they have some sense about them."

"Trouble is, everyone's going to have to be working twice as hard to keep their own beasts safe," Avery said, rubbing his whiskered cheek with the back of his rough hand. "Still and all, we were lucky today, weren't we, Eliza? If it hadn't been for Magen, we would have had ourselves a number of dead sheep to deal with."

Chapter 15
Thoughts of the Future

The work on Creed Farm was beginning to bring out in Magen abilities she had never known she possessed. Not only were Eliza and Avery teaching her more and more about the herds and the mill process, but Eliza had asked Magen to assign and supervise Jane and Emmy's work. It was clear enough that Eliza was slowly grooming Magen to one day take over her job.

Eliza and Avery, who had handled the bulk of the workload themselves during the lean years, had no tolerance for slackers. It was Avery whom most of the workers preferred to work for, because of his wry sense of humor and his uncanny ability to match the right hand to the right job. The chore boys said that "even if you didn't know what you were good at, Avery Mackay could show you within a day's time." Eliza, on the other hand, kept more to herself. She was a fair and stern taskmaster. When she wasn't implementing her own ideas on the farm, she was reading up on the latest theories and practices for improving a farm's yield or a herd's bloodlines. She frequently had her nose in publications like the *Vermont Repository* or the *New England Farmer*. While Creed Farm was not considered large or wealthy, it was fast becoming a "paying farm"—an achievement in itself in hardscrabble Vermont.

After an afternoon spent preparing a bucket of tallow in the firepit for candlemaking the next day, Magen went to collect supplies to stock the medicine cabinet. She was in search of burdock for skin eruptions, and lobelia to make a relaxing tincture. She liked these foraging trips out in the woods on her own. She grabbed her basket and the punctured-tin lantern, in case it got dark. She savored the quiet of the mild late afternoon, hearing only the distant sounds of the sheep as the sun's blanket of warmth began to lift. Magen knew too well how arduous the chores would become in the dead of winter.

Gabriel was working on the roofline of the new barn, and as Magen passed, he jumped down from a ladder to grab a stolen kiss. Magen was so surprised she dropped her basket and pretended to scold him. He knew Avery was close by, so he didn't detain her but he watched Magen as she carried on with her task. She smiled back at him, remembering how he had told her on one of their recent walks that he loved her sense of purpose and self-assurance that other girls lacked. He said that he wished his sister and indeed his own mother had been blessed with "the same strength and sense of purpose the Creed women seem to have." Magen wondered what his sister and mother were like, but Gabriel didn't want to talk about them.

As the sun slipped low in the western sky, Magen stopped on top of the rocky knoll that looked out across the farm; it was one of her favorite spots. Setting her basket of herbs next to her, she admired the blowing fields of corn to the south and the maple sugarbush that glowed from red to brown to gold in the changing light. She spotted Gabriel waving to her from the barn and realized they were probably getting hungry back at the house. She pushed herself up from her perch, grabbed her basket, and with a spring in her step, made her way back to the barn.

Gabe had been working with a long planer, and was smoothing out a board of striped maple. Magen liked to watch him work. She knew the money he was earning from Eliza was important to him. He had an eye on a set of tools for sale in Tucker Gorge. As she approached him, he put his planer down.

"Don't stop. I enjoy watching you work."

The look of appreciation in his eyes warmed her. "Wood is something I understand, I guess. Just as you know your way around a farm."

"Quite a talker, that one," Avery teased, coming up from behind Magen. "Of course, the Creeds aren't exactly known for their chatter either," he said, smiling off Magen's offer to assist him with his water buckets. "Guess I would be the most verbal around here. Wouldn't you agree, young Gabe?"

"I would at that, Mr. Mackay."

Avery was carrying a shoulder yoke with buckets of water up to the house. He cocked an eyebrow in Magen's direction and asked, "Might we be getting some food in us anytime soon, Miss Magen? Or would you care to sit atop your perch out there and contemplate the ways of the world for a bit longer?

Blushing now, Magen laughed, "I'm afraid my thoughts carry me away sometimes. Especially when I can see all of God's creation right up there on the nook."

"Ah, I understand perfectly, lass. Truly, I do. But a mind thinks greater thoughts when its belly is full."

"I'm on my way," Magen laughed, swinging the basket beside her as she strode back to the house.

The late afternoon meal was usually a light one, but even so, Magen felt her mood drop slightly when she took stock of the larder that day. She had been noticing lately that the larder had started to look a bit sparse. There was usually a hung ham or two in there; now, there was only a bit of smoked bacon. The herbs and spices used for cooking and medicines seemed well-enough stocked, but more and more shelves sat empty. Seeing them made Magen remember the lean winters back in Sackitt's Ridge, and a chill went down her arms. She tried not to think too much of it, and hurried back to the bustle of the kitchen.

Chapter 16

The Storm

Six weeks had passed since the day Magen and Gabriel had first ridden in to Creed Farm. Gabriel's work on the barn would soon be complete, and Magen didn't want to think about what came next. The thought of him leaving made her feel physically ill. *How strange,* she thought, *to be so affected by another. I didn't even know him a short time ago. Now it is as though I feel a part of me is missing when he's not around.*

Heading out to the orchard that morning, she spotted him in the field, mending a fence. "Care to help me pick some apples today, Master Gabe?"

"Some people have important work to do, young lady," he teased.

"There are very few things as important as picking apples," Magen replied. Then, steeling her courage, she asked, "Is your family in Bellingham wondering what became of you?"

Gabriel came to a full stop. He looked thoughtful for a moment, then said his father would probably be wondering about him, but his mother would simply be adding his absence to her list of grievances against him.

"And is there no one else to take note of your absence?" Magen asked, trying not to sound too obvious.

Gabriel put his chisel down and walked slowly over to her. He took the long-handled basket out of her hands and placed it on the ground, then he cupped her face in his large rough hands and kissed her firmly on the mouth. The intense look in his eyes caught her off-guard.

She tried to regain her footing, and looked around to see if any other eyes were watching. Gabriel looked down at her with a smile on his face, and then grew more serious. "There is no one in Bellingham or anywhere else who matters to me more than you, Mae Creed. Listen carefully. I love you. I want to be with you today and all the rest of my days."

For one shining moment, time stopped. Magen felt like her heart had forgotten how to beat and her lungs how to breathe. She was weak in the knees and didn't trust her voice, so she grinned, grabbed her basket, and took off for the orchard with her heart soaring. By the time she reached the orchard at the top of the hill, only one thought repeated itself in her head: *He loves me!*

A couple of the young lads whom Avery had hired to help pick the early variety apples were there among the trees. They stood waiting for her to give them instructions, but Magen walked right past them with a broad grin on her face and her thoughts miles away.

"Miss Creed!" a young boy named Brendan shouted. Magen jumped and turned to him.

"You're supposed to tell us where to begin picking."

"Of course," she stammered, commanding herself back to reality. "We'll start on the south end of the orchard. Bring the steps, please." They followed her willingly.

Magen could think of no better chore than to pick apples today. It was one of her favorite things to do, and it meant she could be alone with her thoughts and let her mind wander. With more and more responsibilities falling to her now, the apple picking was a chore she loved to take charge of. Apples were a major part of their diet, and Magen knew well their importance. They baked with them, dried them, roasted them, candied and brandied them. They made apple sauce, apple jack, apple butter, apple cider, and jam. Eliza boasted that Creed Farm had the largest variety of apples of any orchard in the area. Her orchard, which lay near the east boundary of the farm, contained gnarled old trees with delightful names like Baldwins, Pippins, and Sweet Astrachans. Magen had strict instructions to pick only the special crop of August Sweets for the family today. These she would carefully hang to dry with string from the kitchen attic ceiling; that way, they would last longer. What the household didn't eat, they would use for barter at the general store in Saint Rock.

Still relishing Gabe's words, Magen climbed high on the ladder in order to disappear into the limbs of a tree at the end of a row. The apples were redder than usual against a sky that was a flawless blue. She grabbed one and took a bite and knew that it was the best-tasting apple she would ever eat. Nothing could compare to this day!

Possibly even better than the look and taste of an apple, Magen thought, was the aroma of an apple pie baking in the small oven, or the great yellow Pound Sweets which were baked a golden brown and added to the johnny-cakes for Sunday supper. She had built a fire with pine knots in their small brick oven last evening to prepare for the baking later today.

Tomorrow she would help in the long, strenuous process of making apple butter by making a reduction of some of the smaller pitted fruit in an iron pot with a long-handled applewood stirrer over an open fire. It was hot, tedious work, but with any luck, by the end of the day Magen could fill dozens of odd-sized jars to stock the larder.

Magen and the farm lads had started picking at about ten in the morning; Eliza joined them a little later, then Gabriel. They all had bushel baskets underneath their wooden steps, and they were trying to fill them before the heavy gray clouds creeping up from the western horizon emptied out on them.

After perhaps an hour, Magen became aware of a distressed-looking Eliza. She was looking at Gabriel and gesturing toward the horizon, which had suddenly filled up with a dark wall of clouds. Magen saw the billowing black clouds moving rapidly toward them. The pickers became aware of the winds picking up around them, and the flashes of lightning and sounds of thunder—no longer off in the distance, but ominously overhead. They all climbed down from their wooden perches as the rain began to fall. It was no ordinary rain, Magen noticed with alarm. Huge fat drops splattered their faces and pounded them on the head. It felt like an attack on all of them and the precious, bountiful harvest they had just been picking.

Within minutes, the winds picked up to gale force. All of the workers ran for cover. Magen and Eliza made it under the eaves of the sheep barn and looked back at the orchard; never had they seen such a destructive wind. The sheer power of it tore at the trees and roared in their ears. Magen grabbed Eliza's hand as they watched the storm terrorize the orchard and the rest of Creed Farm. Large branches were torn off and blown everywhere, along with anything else unsecured. The sheep protested the needle-like rain on their heads and backs. Huddled together, their loud bleating could barely be heard over the ferocious wind and thunder still passing directly overhead. The shaken young farm hands tried to calm the panic-stricken animals. Everyone tried to maintain safe harbor from the winds, which were not abating.

Gesturing to Magen to take cover in the lower hayloft, Eliza went to find Avery. Magen yelled back that she would see to the horses.

Gabriel, coming up from behind, yelled "Stay put! I'll see to the animals!" When Magen continued to head in the direction of the horses, Gabe turned and took her by the arm. He guided her over to a small stall in the rear of the barn where a baby goat was tethered. Magen could see the animal's terror. "Try to calm her down, Magen." Then he quickly kissed her on the lips. Magen watched him leave as she took the goat in her arms. *God, watch over him,* she thought. The storm continued in varying intensity for the rest of that terrifying afternoon.

When things began to calm down, everyone ventured from their protective shelters to assess the damage. Creed Farm looked like a battlefield. Whole trees had been uprooted. The orchard's beautiful harvest now covered the ground, pummeled and soggy. Corn stalks lay beaten down and broken in the fields. Lake-like puddles stood in the pumpkin patch, and the animals all showed signs of distress.

The storm had moved on before major structural damage had occurred to the house, and only one of the outbuildings had been damaged by a fallen tree. Windows, roof tiles, door hinges, and fences were all that appeared damaged. They didn't know the number of sheep that had been lost yet, but no human life had been taken. From the look of it, a few of the work hands had suffered minor injuries and had been sent to the house to be looked after by Emmy and Jane.

As they would hear later, Creed Farm fared better than most of the farms in the area. The Great September Gale of 1815, as it would eventually be called, hit sporadically in Vermont, and its path of destruction bisected most of New England. Unbeknownst to the bedraggled company of Creed Farm, a relentless march by mother nature had begun.

Chapter 17

Avery Mackay

It took long days of wearying work to clean up the debris left from the storm. Nothing could be done about the ruined corn fields or the damaged apple trees. A large percentage of the apple crop had been stripped from the tree branches before it had had a chance to ripen. What apples they could save were pitted and soggy but would be used nonetheless. Eliza was grateful for the fact that they had picked some of the early crop before the storm hit. She tried to put on a good face in front of the farm crew, but Magen could tell she and Avery were worried.

"I have been blessed with two good, strong carpenters," Eliza said one evening just after the storm. "My new barn stands strong and true and we'll soon mend the rest." Magen understood that if the owner was optimistic, the hired help would be as well. The feeling of relief was palpable.

Magen studied an exhausted Eliza and Avery as they all shared a brew of hot cider around the kitchen hearth one evening not long after the storm. Although concern for the farm and the harvest was on everyone's minds, Magen couldn't help but be curious about the relationship between her aunt and Avery Mackay. She also wondered if perhaps her own presence had changed things between them in any way. It didn't seem likely that there was any romance between Eliza and Avery because of the difference in their stations in life; Avery was Eliza's hired man. Still, they were approximately the same age, Magen guessed, and she could remember a few more oddly-paired couples back in Sackitt's Ridge. Just as she pondered the question further, Magen noticed Avery had caught her looking at him. Their eyes met, and she quickly looked away out of embarassment.

After they finished their cups of cider, Gabriel and Aunt Eliza both decided to retire early to their beds. Magen cleaned the cups and spotted Avery smoking his pipe out on the front porch; she went to join him.

Not being sure how to approach the subject, she began, "Avery, it is none of my business, but—"

"What is the feeling that lies between your aunt and me? Is that what you're wondering, lass?"

"You don't miss much, do you?" Magen grinned.

"You're not the first to wonder, is all," Avery grinned back. "Usually I don't bother to explain, as it's no one else's business. But since you are a Creed and a friend I will tell you all about it." His brogue became more pronounced as he relaxed.

"You seem to be good friends," Magen prompted.

"We are good mates, that is so. But Eliza Creed is not one to wear her heart on her sleeve, if you know what I mean. We have weathered much together, but in the end, she is my employer and owner of this farm. Of that I never lose sight. I started out as a sailor, Magen," Avery said, warming to his story as he leaned back on his elbows, his pipe bowl cupped in his large powerful hand. "As a young lad, my family immigrated from Edinburgh and settled in Portsmouth, New Hampshire. When I was seventeen, my Da got the influenza and died, leaving me and my Ma on our own. She wasn't as strong as she might have been and against my wishes she decided to move us in with her sister's family. I was too old anyway to be living under her wing, so when she got settled, I did what I had long wanted to do—I went to sea.

"I'm not much to look at, I know," he continued, emphasizing the long "o" in his deep Scottish voice. "I was always this tall and lanky. But I knew the sea and I were meant for each other. It didn't take me long to learn my way around a ship, Magen. God—how I loved it! I was living what I thought was the best of lives—not that much older than you are now.

"Then one night the ship I was serving on had made port in London. A mate and I had gone into a tavern and later, on our way back to our ship, we were hit from behind. We had been shanghaied."

"Shanghaied? What does that mean?" Magen asked.

"It's what the Brits called *impressment*—forcing American seamen to serve on British ships. Or, like me, knocked senseless from behind and taken to one of their ships to serve against my will. I was just one of many who suffered that fate. I never saw them coming, or going for that matter. Next thing I knew I was serving under a British captain who was pure evil. I don't say that lightly, Magen. He was a bad man."

"How horrible!" Magen exclaimed.

"It was three years before I made it back to my home. By that time, my mother had died without ever knowing what had become of her only child. And there was a lass I had been sweet on—she had married another."

Magen was shocked and riveted.

"I was angry and couldn't get over the unfairness of it all," Avery continued. "I began to seek comfort in drink, and before long it was the drink that shanghaied me. I drifted here and there, and finally ended up in Vermont in the summer of 1781. You could say Vermont and I were trying to establish ourselves as independent entities at the same time, only Vermont fared better at it."

"What did you do?" Magen asked.

"I spent years doing odd jobs on farms and such, but never lasted anywhere for very long. I missed the sea, but I had no wish to serve on another man's ship and was in no shape to captain one of my own.

"One day, Eliza Creed comes sauntering into Tucker. I was sitting outside the general store, half drunk, half asleep. She stood there in front of me and said in that clear, authoritative way she has that she needed help on her farm, and since I didn't seem to be too occupied she would hire me for the job—just like that. She assumed I would jump at it. Which, of course, I did. At first I thought I'd landed myself an easy position—working for a woman. I was soon disposed of that notion, as well you can imagine."

Magen couldn't picture any other woman being as bold as her Aunt Eliza.

"I don't know why she chose to pick on me, I can say that much," Avery said, laughing. "Later, after I had been here awhile, it occurred to me what a chance she had taken hiring me. My credentials, you might say, did not speak well of my character. And, well, you can imagine the talk in the small village here. But none of that seemed to bother our Eliza. What's more, she paid me for my work. That clinched it, you see. Farmers I worked for would pay me off with a bottle and a by-your-leave, if at all. But Eliza Creed insisted on paying me wages. That was more than eight years ago. I haven't had a drink since."

Hearing his story, Magen felt a strong affection for him and for her aunt as well. She thought it unusual to find a man who didn't need to be the hero in his own story. She liked him for his honesty and wanted to know more, but Avery grinned in that lopsided way he had. He tapped his pipe bowl on the bottom of his boot to empty the ash, and hoisted himself up off the step as if to signal the conversation was over. In his slow, deliberate way he turned to Magen and said, "I'm pleased you've come here, Magen Creed. You have a pure heart and you're good for our Eliza."

Magen smiled, touched by his words, and like the very first time she met him, she saw the wisdom and kindness in his eyes. She watched him walk toward his bunk in one of the outbuildings, and Magen found herself wondering anew about the nature of his feelings toward Eliza. Was he in love with her? He never actually said.

Chapter 18

An Excursion

While Magen awoke at dawn most mornings, Eliza was almost always awake before her, nursing the fire in the hearth and preparing something hot to drink. This morning though, Magen lay upstairs listening to the sounds of the old house creaking in the autumn winds. Not wanting to leave the warmth of her feather bed, she hugged her quilt closer. The unique pattern on the bride's quilt had been created by her Grandmother Lavinia Magen. Uninvited memories began to tug at the back of her brain as she lay there—the terrible mornings waking up in the pest house; the sounds and smell of sickness.

Magen realized with an incredible sadness that she couldn't get a clear picture of Carrie's face in her mind's-eye anymore. How awful, that she could forget her sister like that. She could picture her father clearly. But images of Sara and Carrie were harder to bring into focus. Hearing her aunt downstairs, Magen got up and tried to shake off bleak images from the past. She took her homespun dress from its hook beside the bed, and feeling her goosebumps rise, pulled it over the cotton chemise she had slept in. She slipped on her leather flats and left the cold room with its sad thoughts for the warmth of the kitchen hearth.

Just as she knew she would, Magen found Eliza bustling around the kitchen, preparing the morning coffee, and slicing the hard bread. After saying their good mornings, Eliza poured Magen her mug of steaming coffee. It had taken a while to get used to her aunt's strong coffee. Sara had always served tea. But Magen now depended on that first kick of the brew to face the day's work.

Watching her aunt move around the kitchen "tending to things," as she put it, Magen noticed that Eliza never wasted a moment. Every move was efficient and focused. Eliza never showed vulnerability, at least not in front of others. It must have come from the path she had chosen in life, but Eliza needed to look in charge and in control of everything at all times. Magen guessed that Eliza thought being vulnerable somehow made one weak. And Eliza would never allow herself to appear weak. Magen wished her aunt could let her guard down now and again. Perhaps she didn't realize something Magen had already learned—it was people's weaknesses that made them human and more accessible to others.

"We're having a bit of a holiday today, Magen," Eliza declared, and her voice snapped Magen out of her thoughts. "The hired hands will take care of the farm chores, so no need to don your work clothes. Just grab a wrap and we'll be off to town."

"Town? Aunt Eliza! How exciting! What's the occasion?"

"The occasion is that I have put it off long enough. I need supplies, and it's time you see something of the area. We won't go as far as Tucker. What we need, we can get here in Saint Rock. In the past, at least when we had a good year, we would go with the Reynolds to Portsmouth, New Hampshire. We would fill the oxcart with our wares and off we went. Some years we had quite a long line of wagons and sleds loaded down with goods. The ships came in from all over to Portsmouth.

"That must have been a sight to see," Magen said.

"We purchased a plow for Avery one year—getting it back here was a mighty feat. This year there'll be no such trip, the weather has seen to that. I can't remember the last time we had such a meager harvest. Still, I'll not brood over it—too much to do."

Since arriving there, Magen had not given a great deal of thought to the world outside of Creed Farm. But she was excited to be presented now with the opportunity for an excursion. Although she and Gabriel had ridden through it the day they arrived, her mind had been too occupied to pay Saint Rock much heed.

As the morning sun began to move higher in the sky, Avery and Gabriel joined the two women in the kitchen for their morning coffee. Eliza offered them a quick meal of bread and the leftover stew from the night before. Pieces of the dried salt pork had enhanced the flavor. Eliza said she wanted to be on their way to town as soon as possible so they wouldn't "waste" an entire day at the market.

Magen rushed through her stew and excused herself to go back upstairs. She decided she wanted to look more presentable, if she could. Most days, she wore her long black hair tucked up under a cap or plaited into a braid that hung down her back, but today she decided to brush it out and let it fall over her shoulder. Sara used to spend an inordinate amount of time fixing her own and Carrie's hair into sausage curls, which, according to Miss Wordleave, was the way townsfolk wore it. Magen thought it funny that people would try and emulate total strangers.

Upstairs, Magen put her woolen cloak on over her cotton shirtwaist. Realizing the cloak was much too warm for the day, she took it off again and flung it over her arm. By the time she got out the front door she was surprised to see Avery and Gabriel already mounted on their horses and Eliza was climbing aboard the wagon. Magen could see that Aunt Eliza, while not wasting time on fashioning her hair, had at least conceded to some form of fashion by donning a dress. It was a plain cotton homespun, and Magen couldn't help feeling a little relieved that it wasn't her usual breeches and dirty linen work smock.

"I'm fodder for the town's gossip, as it is. Don't need to draw more attention to myself by wearing my usual garb," Eliza nodded.

It had been decided that Gabriel would go with them to Saint Rock and then continue on to Windmill Point where he had to see to some unfinished business. While there, he would retrieve Magen's wagon, which had remained with Gabe's friend who owned the ferry boat. Magen had little enough need now for the items in the wagon, but it would be good to have it back all the same.

While Gabriel took care of his errands, Avery and Magen would help Eliza purchase the supplies they needed in Saint Rock. According to Avery, Eliza would put off "town days" for as long as possible. "When she can't put it off any longer, we go with a list as long as your two arms," he laughed.

Chapter 19

Grandfather and Grandmother Creed

"Come on now, Betsy," Eliza coaxed the old horse over the rutted dirt path. "It'll be easier going once we're on the stone-filled post road. It goes all the way into Tucker Gorge, now."

While Avery followed behind Eliza's wagon, Gabriel rode up alongside Magen, tipped his hat and smiled at her before taking off ahead of them. Eliza noticed that Magen watched long after Gabriel's horse disappeared from view.

"Betsy knows the way so well we can just sit back and enjoy the warm sun on our face, Magen," Eliza sighed and settled back with the reins held loosely in her hands. Magen decided to take advantage of the opportunity to have Aunt Eliza alone and away from farm business.

"What sort of people were your Pa and Ma, Aunt Eliza?" she asked.

"When Pa was around, Pa was in charge. Of that there was never any doubt. He rode roughshod over Ma, same as he did with us. The only person who wasn't afraid of our Pa was your Pa. I reckon he had Pa's true measure. Our Pa would bring the wrath of God down on Samuel, and Samuel would hand it right back. He was the only person I ever knew who didn't let Pa intimidate him. Ma would tremble in his wake, as most people did. Samuel, though, was different. Pa would be railing on him something fierce, and Samuel would just stare at him, no visible expression whatsoever—so you wouldn't know what he was thinking. It would drive Pa into a frenzy. One time after Pa had been savage toward him, Samuel told me to take no heed. 'It's all smoke and mirrors' he said—'just smoke and mirrors.'

"I never forgot that. It made me see our Pa in a different light from then on. He was more of a performer than anything. That's why he was so good at preaching."

Magen realized Eliza was recalling things she hadn't in a very long time, so she thought better of interrupting.

"I don't think our Ma ever wanted to leave Massachusetts, but of course she did Pa's bidding. After uprooting Ma from the only home she had ever known, Pa decided that he missed riding the preachers'circuit, and didn't much like being tied down to the demands of a hardscrabble farm."

"What did he look like?" Magen asked.

"Big, tall, a chiseled, dark face—in his later years, a shock of white hair. When he got to preaching, sometimes he looked like he was possessed by some unearthly spirit."

"It's not surprising people were a bit afraid of him then," Magen said. "I'm not sure I would have liked Grandfather much, considering how he treated Pa."

"Well Samuel was right, our Pa was a consummate actor. It was a shame Ma never understood that. She was a quiet, sad little thing. But she loved going to the meeting house here in Saint Rock—two or three times a week she went. It wasn't that she was so devout; she just loved the singing," Eliza said, and shook her head in a puzzled way.

"I don't know how it was where you came from Magen. Here, Deacon Hitchcock would line out a psalm and the congregation would sing after him. It took the patience of Job to get through those services. But Ma took great comfort in it, somehow."

Magen smiled to remember some of the interminably long services she had sat through with Sara at the Sackitt's Ridge meeting house.

"She didn't have strong maternal feelings, our Ma. But she wasn't unkind to Samuel and me," Eliza said without bitterness.

"Like Pa, though, she was no farmer; that much they had in common. As I said, Pa liked the idea of being a farmer. Fortunately the farm had been lovingly and diligently cared for by its original owners. It was able to survive our Pa and the men he later hired to run it. I often thought that if he had just let Samuel take over the running of things, Samuel never would have left. But Pa wouldn't hand over the reins. And Samuel was too impatient; he couldn't wait it out. He and Ruth were anxious to make their own mark in this world."

"And my Ma? What was she like?"

"She was as strong-willed as Samuel. And had an independent spirit, like you do, Magen. While my brother was more intelligent than our Pa, he was just as stubborn. They were just like two bulls with their horns stuck. They had one too many disagreements and the day came when Samuel had had enough. He and Ruth started dreaming of going to the West.

Ruth would have followed Samuel anywhere. They were married with Ma's blessing, but they didn't tell Pa. After they discovered she was carrying you they decided to head out."

"Didn't your Ma try to stop them? Didn't you?"

"Ma didn't know Ruth was pregnant nor did she know of their plans to leave. I tried my best to talk Samuel into being patient. When Pa died the farm would be his. But even Ruth was anxious to go. They were dreamers, the two of them."

"It doesn't seem a practical thing to do when you know you are expecting a child," Magen said.

"They were planning on leaving one morning in late August, but somehow Pa learned of their plans. In their last confrontation, Samuel told Pa to leave the farm to me. He said he and Ruth would raise their family on their own farm out West. That's what Samuel said. I don't know if you can imagine the kind of temper our Pa had, Magen; I hope you never experience such a thing. Pa tried to beat some sense into Samuel, and for the first time Samuel didn't fight back."

Magen could see Eliza was having difficulty continuing.

"Samuel and Ruth left that day. And I never saw my brother again."

"How terrible for Pa—for you both," Magen said. "No wonder he didn't like talking about his father."

"I got the farm by default, Magen. Pa would never have bequeathed it to me—I was only a daughter, after all. The tragedy is that he only lived two more years. And Ruth ended up having you early, long before they reached the West."

"They never even came close," Magen said sadly.

The wheels creaking over the uneven road and the slow movement of the wagon should have lulled Magen into a sleepy calm, but she was unsettled by the conversation.

"You said Samuel later took to smuggling, didn't you, child?" Eliza asked, interrupting Magen's thoughts.

"Yes. That's the last time I saw him. More than two years ago now. I know Sara believed Pa was killed, and I guess she's probably right that he's dead. Still, there's a part of me that believes he just might still be alive somewhere."

The two women were quiet for awhile, alone with their own thoughts and memories of Samuel Creed. Magen shared her discovery of Ruth's grave and of the Ables' kindness, and Eliza was as impressed by the serendipity of the experience as Magen had been.

"Do you believe in God, Aunt Eliza?" Magen asked after a bit.

After some time without answering, Eliza said, "Creed Farm is what I know of God, Magen. And all I ever need to know."

Chapter 20

Saint Rock

When they arrived in Saint Rock, Avery helped Magen and Eliza down from their seats. Gabe continued on to Windmill Point, waving and hollering "Goodbye and good luck!" over his shoulder. Magen smiled after him. Avery left the horse and wagon tied in front of the general store and said he'd get started hauling in the crates. The folks walking by appeared friendly enough, throwing curious glances in Magen's direction. She liked it when Eliza introduced her to some of them with a note of pride in her voice.

"Sackitt's Ridge had a general store but it wasn't as interesting as this one," Magen said as they walked into the dimly lit, cavernous store. Instead of windows, which would have brightened the place, each wall was covered floor-to-ceiling with shelves heaped with goods of every description. The effect was cozy and welcoming.

Rakes, spades, and baskets hung from the ceiling. Glass cabinets of spices, teas, tinned goods, and colorful candies lined the wall behind where the merchant stood. In the back of the store, a group of farmers sat playing a game of checkers next to a coal-burning stove.

"If we don't get a break in the weather soon, these wolves are going to have all of our herds for scraps," one farmer yelled at another.

Avery walked over to the dispirtied-looking lot. "Gentlemen," he said. "I can hear from your voices you've received the same visitors that we have. We're not usually fighting our four-legged foes at this time of year. There's truth in that, sure enough. But working together, I'm sure we'll be able to slow down the carnage."

"It's a sorry state having to talk wolf bounties this early in the season," one farmer grumbled as he gnashed down on a cigar butt. Magen watched Avery nod his agreement and tip his hat to them before returning to the wagon outside. Eliza was reviewing her list of needed supplies with the store merchant, Mr. McRedmond, so Magen decided to assist Avery in bringing from the wagon what they intended to use in trade. Jars of honey, bricks of beeswax, eggs, bags of wool from last spring, and a few pecks of apples. "Not our normal haul," Avery said with a sigh.

"Better than most," Mr. McRedmond assured Eliza. "The storm's affected nearly every family this year, and everyone's needs are greater than their haul. I fear we're in for a very long winter."

After their purchases had been made, Magen and Eliza left the McRedmond's Store and told Avery they would meet him down at the blacksmith's, where he had left his horse to be shod. Eliza nodded at the merchants and a few passersby. Magen was surprised when more than one young- and not-so-young-a-man tipped his hat at her aunt. Magen could feel curious stares follow them as they moved along the walkway. She thought it must be an occasion when Eliza Creed came to town for people to take such notice.

⟡

The three weary travelers returned home to Creed Farm that evening and entered the house weighted down with packages of spices, a set of two chambersticks, a copper kettle, boots for Avery, a night cap and bedsheets for Eliza, a packet of sewing needles, and a fake ivory hair comb for Magen that she got to choose herself. Avery had other packages of tools and animal feed he would unload the next day. All of them remarked on the fatigue they felt. It was Eliza's opinion that the fatigue came more from the stress of being away from the farm all day than from the exertion of shopping.

Eliza tasted the contents of the aromatic stew pot and swung the kettle on its crane back towards the fire. "Ah. Better than common, I should say. We'll wait on Gabriel to return before we sit down to eat."

"I should think he'll be along, directly," Avery said.

No sooner had he spoken than they heard Gabriel's horse gallup up the road. Magen went to the door to greet him, with a feeling of delight as she saw his tall figure walking toward her. Hat in hand, he smiled down at her and they snuck in a kiss before Eliza or Avery noticed.

"And how was your day in Saint Rock, Mae? Did you dazzle all whom you met?"

Feeling her face flush, Magen smiled back and answered that they had had a grand day in town. Gabriel and Magen entered the kitchen and Avery greeted Gabe with a smile; even Eliza was warm to him, Magen noticed.

"I regret having to disrupt your fine meal. But I have some unfortunate news," Gabriel said in a serious tone. "Word had been left in Rouses Point for me that my Pa has taken a turn for the worse. I must be off to Bellingham in the morning. I don't know how long I'll be gone. My Ma is in need of me, and I will have to stay until things are settled with them." A silence filled the room for many moments.

"Of course you must go, Gabriel," Aunt Eliza said standing up to fix him a bowl of stew. Noticing Magen's crestfallen face, Eliza added, "We wouldn't dream of keeping you from your family obligations, would we, Magen?"

Magen felt a hollow space in the pit of her stomach, but she shook her head. She remained silent, because she was afraid she would start crying if she tried to say anything. Registering Magen's reaction, Eliza continued, "I wager there will still be work here for you when you return."

"Aye, I can vouch for that, lad," Avery said.

Looking around at the concern in their eyes, Gabriel said, "My father was once a proud soldier. But his war took everything he had to give. He's never been one to complain, so I shouldn't either. Besides, my mother does enough of that for us all. She— well, let's just say she has never adjusted well to having an invalid for a husband."

"I'm sorry, Gabriel. It must be difficult for all of you. Is there anything I can do?" Magen asked.

Looking intensely at her, he responded without hesitation, "Be here when I return." And with that he walked out.

Eliza, standing there holding the bowl of uneaten stew, looked from Magen to Avery. "This doesn't bode well for that family. I met his mother once. She'll be looking for ways to keep her son close by, if heaven should see fit to finally take his Pa."

"You think he might be unable to return to us, aunt?" Magen asked, hoping they didn't hear the alarm in her voice.

Eliza looked at Magen with concern in her eyes. "He has an obligation to his family, Magen. They come before all else."

Chapter 21

Early Winter

The warm glow of the passing autumn evolved into the stark blues and grays of a New England November. The dark descended early now; first the wind stirred the brown dead leaves, then the rain made a heavy mat of them. Magen loved the way the light played on the hillsides. The sharp, lush colors of summer were replaced now by the soft, subtle hues of the dark time of year. With the leaves off the trees, vast openings were created in the landscape that were not there before. It opened one's eyes to a different kind of beauty.

This year felt different, though, Magen thought, as she hiked to the east meadow over a field of dead straw. The craggy bare tree limbs silhouetted against the low winter sky stirred something deep inside her—a melancholy she had never experienced before. There was a fragility to this time of the year just before the snows came.

The September Gale, which people were still talking about, had created more work and heartache for them all. The orchard looked different—defaced, damaged. It filled her with a foreboding she could not name. Grateful for the work that kept her busy, Magen refused to let herself be depressed.

While Avery saw to the pruning and removal of the damaged trees, Magen assisted Aunt Eliza in checking and repairing the fence lines between pastures. She had noticed that Eliza seemed to grow tired more easily of late. Magen blushed to recall a conversation she overheard the other night between her aunt and Avery. She knew she shouldn't have listened, but she did anyway. And although she had felt guilty eavesdropping, she was also relieved to know that at least *she* wasn't the cause of Eliza's worries these days.

"You were right, Avery. The two young ones do know themselves, after all," was the way Eliza had put it to Avery. "As individuals, they're resolute; together, they seem a real force."

Avery had made a gutteral response of approval to this comment and then he had added, "Gabe's intelligent. He understands the dignity of Magen."

"And it's a rare man who makes a practice of that," Eliza said ruefully, then softened her response, "I've only ever experienced it with you, Avery." Avery didn't say anything then, which Magen thought spoke volumes.

It was recalling the rest of their conversation that made Magen uneasy as she tramped through the field thinking about it.

"I'm not one to hold with bad omens or fortune telling," Eliza had said. "But lately I've had a sense of foreboding that I can neither identify nor dismiss." Avery had not shrugged off Eliza's anxieties; instead, he had reassured her that Gabriel would return soon, and they would all weather together whatever was to come.

Magen made it out to the pasture's fenceline now and awaited Eliza, whom she could see in the distance coming toward her.

"What is it, Eliza? You look concerned."

"Oh, Magen. I'm just remembering back to the lean years when Avery and I had so little. Now our abundance—well, it takes my breath away. I don't welcome lean times back to Creed Farm. Even though I know life is a balancing act, I much prefer the bounty I've come to love than the scarcity I once knew so well."

"Sophia Able said something like that to me, Eliza. You and Avery have inherited the history of one another and this place, just like the Ables. I think it's what makes you both strong."

"Yes, that's true," Eliza said, chewing on a piece of straw and looking off into the distance. "Since the storm, though, all Avery and I talk about is just surviving this winter."

Magen tried to smile and linked her arm with Eliza's. "We need to check that the grain harvest has been seen to in the upper loft. Come, Aunt."

They entered the sweet smelling loft of the big barn. Inside, two of the young chore boys were still hard at work, facing each other over a sheaf with flail staffs in hand—one stepping forward while the other stepped backward across the puncheon floor, beating the grain from its stalk in the dust-filled air.

"We're behind our work, Magen," Eliza fretted. "This should have been done already. But at least the wheat and corn is in—what survived the storm, anyway. Let's finish our fence and find Avery."

After working side-by-side pounding sharpened chestnut fence posts and restacking the oak rails into the hard ground, Magen and Eliza made their way up to Avery who had been overseeing the digging of a pit behind the barn. Every year a pit was dug just below the frost line, Eliza explained to Magen, and filled with extra fruit and root crops from the harvest. These buried provisions would later supplement the herd's diet of hay and grain before the spring lambing time.

As Magen and Eliza approached, they saw Avery turn and shake his head as he walked away from the two field hands; concern was written in his furrowed brow.

"What is it?" Eliza asked as they met up with him.

"We're beginning to see just how much of a toll that infernal storm has taken on the farm, Eliza. Now it's plain."

Eliza waited with a silent, questioning look.

"This year the pit will not be so deep, lass."

Chapter 22
Past and Present

"It's a lot easier to keep these creatures happy in the warm months," the shepherd boy named Joe called out to Magen over the bleating of the sheep. The early December morning had a bite to it, and Magen was beginning to wish she hadn't volunteered to help Joe keep an eye out for hungry predators. The wolf attacks had grown more bold in the dawn and twilight recently.

"My Pa swears he can hear a change in the weather coming," Joe called again. "He says we'll have snow by week's end."

"That doesn't surprise me," Magen said. "Avery claims he can predict the size of a coming storm based on how the furniture creaks." Joe grinned at this and guided two ewes over to their youngsters.

The mention of Avery got Magen to wondering how his trip to Bellingham was going. Although he went there to check on grain shipments, he had promised to look in on the Thayer family. Gabriel had been gone for close to a month now and the passage of time didn't make his absence any easier for Magen to bear. Sometimes when Magen entered the newly-finished barn, just the smell of the sawdust would bring thoughts of him so clearly to mind that she would ache with the physical longing of him. She loved him. It was as simple and as complicated a thing as Magen had ever known. She would have liked to talk about these feelings with Aunt Eliza but didn't know how.

Avery also was charged with the purchase of special spices and fruit while in Bellingham. Eliza had been planning for the farm's Thanksgiving Day celebration for weeks now. "This year will be extra special because you're with us Magen. I think everyone needs a day to forget their struggles." Magen was grateful for Eliza's sentiments and looked forward to preparing a meal for friends and neighbors of the Creeds, but she worried about the practicality of planning a feast when the harvest had been so dear. But Thanksgiving was the most important celebration of the year, according to Eliza. "We have more to be grateful for than most," was the way she had put it. So Magen decided to let go of her worries and just hope that Avery would return home soon with news of Gabriel.

"I'm going up to the house, Joe," Magen called with her hand cupped to her mouth. "I'll bring you back something warm to drink later when you break for supper." The easy-going shepherd boy nodded and waved Magen on.

As Magen entered the warm, inviting kitchen Eliza was busy stoking the fire, stirring a pot of beans and counting out jars of jam and honey from the larder.

"I'm glad you're here, Magen. With Jane and Emmy gone home for a few days, it's up to you and me to organize the menu for Thanksgiving supper. Warm yourself and grab a mug of tea. We'll make a start." Magen warmed her backside by the fire and tossed out a few ideas, such as corn pudding, sweet yams, and butternut stew, which Eliza either rejected or embraced with the scratching of a stubby lead pencil.

"I don't remember ever having such a grand Thanksgiving in Sackitt's Ridge, Aunt. Mostly it meant a long day at the meeting house in prayer and sermons."

"That's how I remember the holiday from my childhood, too. I was determined to do it differently when I took over the farm."

Thinking a lot about Gabriel lately, Magen asked Eliza how her parents, Samuel and Ruth had first met.

"One day our Pa sent Samuel to New York to deliver a lease agreement to a farmer there by the name of Severence. Ruth was Severence's niece. They spent a fair amount of time together, Ruth and Samuel. When Samuel returned, that's all he talked about—to me, anyway. 'Ruth this, Ruth that.' In a very short time, she became the beginning and the end for him. Your mother was an unusual girl, Magen. Headstrong, she was, and adventurous; just like you. I think they believed that as long as they were together they could do just about anything. It took a lot of courage for Ruth to leave her home and follow her heart. If only her body had been as strong as her will."

"What was it like after they left? After your folks died?" Magen asked hesitantly.

"I was completely alone after the folks died, and had no way of know-ing how to reach Samuel. I was terrified at first. Much like you must have felt not so long ago. I was afraid to wake up in the morning. But it was the farm that saved me. It needed me. The animals needed seeing to, and the crops had to be planted. I couldn't just let us all starve. I knew I couldn't do it alone, though.

"I had worked out an agreement with some of the neighboring families: a share in our crops for any help they could provide me. Some of them are working for me still. But it wasn't until Avery came full-time that I really believed I could make a go of this place. By and by, weeks turned into months. Then before I knew it, months turned into years. Somehow we survived."

"It must have taken a great deal of courage."

"It wasn't courage, child; it was fear. I often thought your Pa and Ruth had more courage than I—willing to leave their homes and try the unknown."

"Sara never understood why Pa gave up his inheritance," Magen remembered. "It was one of the things they fought about. Pa was always looking for reasons to journey off. It was only because of me that he and Sara were wed in the first place—because he needed help. That explains why they were never happy together."

"Don't go blaming yourself for their unhappiness, Magen. Nobody knows what life has in store for us. We do what we can, that's all. We do what we have to."

Then Eliza did something unexpected. She took Magen's face in her hands and looked her straight in the eye: "You didn't ask to be born, Magen. It wasn't your fault Ruth died, or Sara either. You have done your mother and father proud." Embarrassed by her show of emotion, Eliza let go then and started bustling around the kitchen again.

After a bit, Magen said, "I'm sure most of your neighbors expected you to turn this place over to someone else to run once your folks died, didn't they, Aunt?"

"Until I found Avery, I was often of a mind to do just that," she answered, her hands now busy grinding the cornmeal for tomorrow's bread-making.

"I knew I had to have some help, and, well, men don't like working for women. All the ones I took a chance on either wanted to take over the place or take over me. After living under the yoke of my father, I knew I wouldn't live like that again."

"How is it that you hired Avery? From what he has told me of his past, he wouldn't have seemed so … promising of a choice!"

Eliza laughed at this. "I saw a man who had lost his pride, Magen. He was the perfect choice."

Chapter 23

Thanksgiving and a Reunion

At last, Avery returned from his trip to Bellingham. Magen tried hard not to let her excitement show, but she could hardly wait for news of Gabriel.

Avery pulled the wagon up to the front of the house, and Eliza greeted him. She was excited to inventory the supplies he had brought back for the holiday dinner. The celebration would be in two days' time; the day had been set and neighbors had been invited. Avery had brought sugar, cranberries, and special spices that Jane and Emmy would use in the baking for the feast.

One of the hired field hands had been lucky enough to bag a turkey on a recent early morning hunt. In addition to roasting the bird, they would be butchering a young pig to round out the table. They had just enough root crops and baked apples and potatoes to go around, Eliza estimated. Now the girls needed to get started on the puddings, cakes, and pies.

After the commotion over the food items, everyone got back to their respective chores, but Magen cornered Avery in the barn.

"Oh! You'll be wanting news of young Master Thayer, lass?" Avery teased Magen, but when he saw her earnest expression he didn't have the heart to continue. "Gabriel Thayer is as well as can be expected, Magen. I ran into him in town, as it happened. The first words out of his mouth were to ask after you. I hadn't enough time to get the particulars on his situation, though. But rest your mind: he's well in body, if a bit flattened in spirit. My guess is he'll be put to rights when next he sees you." With a grin and a salute, Avery left to get caught up on his own chores. Magen stood with her arms wrapped about her middle. The words went a long way in comforting her. Still, a note from Gabriel would have been a welcomed sight. She wondered for the thousandth time how long it would be before they saw each other again.

The day of "grateful celebration," as Jane and Emmy called it, dawned cold and gray. There was a hint of snow in the air, but nothing could dampen the enthusiasm of those that gathered at Creed Farm that day. In addition to Eliza, Avery, and Magen, there was Jane, Emmy, and their mother and father and three siblings. Three of the Hart brothers arrived with two of their friends in tow, who looked as though they hadn't had a square meal in months. Later in the day, Eliza's friends and neighbors Louise and George Reynolds were to come by to share a slow pudding.

Eliza and Magen had cleared all unnecessary furnishings from the kitchen, so all that was left was the large walnut trestle table and its benches. Avery and the lads then put together a makeshift extension for the table, by placing long pine planks atop two saw horses. All the food was put on the table about midday. Although there wasn't enough for seconds, everyone received a bountiful serving and was grateful for it.

It was decided that before the desserts were served everyone needed to take a break and work off some of the excitement of the day. Without too much effort, the makeshift tables were dismantled and hauled out onto the porch, leaving enough bare floor space to dance a few reels. The Hart brothers had brought along their fiddles and mouth harp, and for two hours everyone forgot about the bad harvest, the September Gale, and the howling wolves. Eliza made a toast with some of her hard cider, and the baked apple and pumpkin pies were served. Hours after they had arrived, an exhausted but grateful crowd of neighbors shared a carriage ride home. Magen could never remember food tasting so good. The only thing that had been missing was Gabriel.

The next few days were raw and cold. But the warm feeling from their day of celebration stayed with Magen and sustained her. The first big snowfall arrived on December the fifth. Eliza and Avery were both in the barn and Magen was out in the hen house when she heard a soft gallop coming up the road. With her basket half full of eggs, she went to take a look. Magen recognized Toby, Gabriel's beautiful black Morgan, trotting up to the house with a well-clad rider on its back. She went to greet him, her heart beating wildly.

"Magen!" Gabriel called, and his smile sent goose bumps up her arms. Reaching out for her hand as he slid down from the saddle, he looked her in the eyes and they gave each other a passionate kiss. Before either of them could say more, Avery came up and grabbed the horse's lead rope; Eliza was close behind him.

"How goes it, young Gabriel? Is the family doing all right then?" Avery asked.

"My Pa passed away just after I saw you in Bellingham, Avery. His old war injuries finally got the better of him," Gabriel said, not taking his eyes off Magen. "Still and all, I reckon I can be thankful I had my Pa for as long as I did. He was a good father to me. And I'll miss him."

"We're so sorry for your loss, Gabriel," Eliza said, and Avery nodded. A moment passed in silence.

"Still, it is good to see you back, laddie. I dare say our Magen has felt your absence. Haven't you, lass?"

Magen could feel herself blush, and, of course, that made her blush all the more. She wished just once she could greet Gabriel without Avery and Eliza hovering so close. Gabe, meanwhile, stared at Magen unabashedly and smiled as though he couldn't stop; he was oblivious to any onlookers.

"Your mother and sister must be at a loss, I should think," Eliza said, steering Gabriel away from Magen and leading him toward the house.

"Without my father to tend to, my mother and Adele would like to move back to Boston from where my mother's family hails. They'll be devoting themselves full time now to acquiring a husband for Adele. He must, of course, be a man of means," Gabe said in a mocking, puffed-up tone. "Mother can now accuse me of abandonment. But being cooped up in that mausoleum of a house one day longer was more than I had it in me to do."

Magen did not want to appear too anxious, but she ventured to ask, "Will you be returning to them then?" Gabriel's look turned dark as he considered the question.

"It was a disappointment of a husband she had, my mother said often enough. Now she's waiting to see if her son will prove any better." With that he shrugged and turned away. Magen felt uncomfortable with Gabe's words and noticed that Eliza did, too.

Over the next few days, the household took up its former rhythms of work and meals, plus the added delight of being in each other's company once more. But Magen didn't believe things were as before. She could see Gabriel's unease at times. She knew that he may be called back to Bellingham. Although neither spoke of it, they both knew their time together was determined by someone else's by-your-leave.

Eliza and Avery, aware that there were few forces on earth as powerful as first love, seemed to give Magen and Gabriel some space.

One afternoon, after her chores had been seen to, Magen went out to check the skeps in the orchard. The bees became dormant through most of the winter, but she looked in on them from time to time to make sure predators weren't tampering with the hives. From the orchard she hiked over to her favorite knoll that overlooked the farm. Here she felt a deep abiding calm. The late afternoon sun would soon turn to the cold of a December evening, and the deep navy streaks of the winter sky were spliced with silver and gold. The horizon provided just the right backdrop to highlight the intricate silhouettes of the leafless trees.

While many complained about the bitter cold of the long northern winters, Magen held this time close to her. She found a connection to this wild, unforgiving land and a clarity to this season that brought her a sense of well-being and peace.

Magen saw Gabe walking up the path toward her. It was as if her spirit had called to him. She watched his approach, acutely aware now of the ache he stirred inside her. She smiled and put out her hand to assist him up the rocky ledge. He clasped her hand and let out a deep sigh—like releasing weeks of pent-up worry and stress. Neither spoke. They sat there together close, sides touching. They felt each other's warmth as they watched the winter sun settle into home.

Chapter 24

Goodbye Again

Magen and Gabe spent every free moment together over the next few days. Snow fell on Friday but did not accumulate. Saturday morning, Magen prepared meat pies for that evening's dinner. The small brick oven to the side of the giant hearth was white-hot from the burning pine knots she had laid the night before. As she rolled out the dough, she heard a rider come up the drive. She looked out and saw a man on a horse. Gabriel, who had been working in the barn, walked toward him. Magen wiped her hands on her apron and went to the front door to get a better look.

She saw Gabriel's look of concern as the man, still mounted, spoke to him. He rode away without ever dismounting. Gabriel noticed Magen for the first time as she came out onto the porch.

"I thought my mother would give me more time, Magen. But I must return to Bellingham," he said slowly. He reached out for her hand. "Mother says she is ill and needs me there. My sister is incapable of handling things on her own. And as my mother takes pleasure in reminding me, I promised my dying father that I would look after them." At this point there was anger in his voice and his grip on Magen's hand tightened.

Magen responded quietly, "A promise is a promise, Gabriel. I understand that you must go." Gabriel bent over her and just as he was about to kiss her, Eliza came out the front door. Gabe sighed in frustration.

"News from home, Gabriel?" Eliza asked.

"Yes. With regret, I'll be off as soon as this day's work is done." Gabe looked at Magen with utter despair, then turned and walked off. Magen returned to the house, brushing past Aunt Eliza's attempt to console.

The rest of the day was a blur of work. Magen prepared a huge meal for that evening, with dishes she didn't normally make. She knew that she wouldn't have the appetite to eat, but she wanted to do something for Gabriel before he left, and he was certainly dearer to her than her concern about the harvest.

Aunt Eliza returned at candlelight and commented on the amount of food. But seeing the dispirited look on Magen's face, she decided not to say anything more. She could see how hard Magen was working to contain her emotions.

With the work done at last, they all came in and sat down to what had turned into a veritable feast. It was cold with a wet falling snow outside, but the kitchen was toasty warm from the fire which had been burning hotter than usual all day. Unfortunately none of them had the appetite to do justice to the meal Magen had spent hours on, nor energy enough for conversation to make it feel like a normal dinnertime. Magen excused herself early and went upstairs to her room. She watched from her bedroom window as Gabriel made his way to his bed in the outbuilding behind the barn.

She tossed and turned for hours. She could not let go of the fact that Gabriel would be leaving in the morning. It was a two-day ride to Bellingham, and Magen didn't know when or if he would be back. Finally she got up and wrapped her woolen shawl around her shoulders. She took her chamber stick to light the way, and slipped downstairs. Not wanting to awaken Aunt Eliza, she tiptoed to the front door in her light leather flats and cringed at the creaking sound the front door made pushing against the steady December wind.

Without a clear thought except that she had to see Gabe, Magen made her way to the outbuilding. When she let herself in and saw him sitting on his cot wide awake she knew he was waiting for her and she knew what they were about to do. She went over to him.

Gabe stood up and took the candle from her hand. He set it down on the wooden crate next to his cot. "You shouldn't be here, Mae," he said in a hoarse whisper.

"I come with a full heart, Gabriel. Just as I am old enough to know my own mind. I pledge both my mind and heart to you for as long as we both live."

"Are you sure of this, Mae? Because I will not ask again."

She placed her hand firmly in his as her answer.

Gabriel wrapped his hands around Mae's. "My father told me once of a long-ago practice called 'handfasting.' Christians could become betrothed with a pledge and a handshake. I pledge my life to you tonight, Magen," he said, tightening his grip around her hands.

Magen felt no hesitation. As she knew that she was a part of Creed Farm, so too she knew that she and this man belonged together.

His kiss, at first soft and gentle, soon turned powerful, urgent. For the first time since meeting one another, Gabriel and Magen could completely let down their guard. Her need for him was as strong as his for her. He was exactly as she knew he would be—gentle, strong, respectful and loving.

With tears in her eyes from the sheer joy that his body brought to hers, Magen gave herself over completely to someone she loved beyond all thought, beyond all worry—to the feel of him holding her in his strong arms, and the way he stroked the small of her neck. Magen knew she had dreamed of this moment from the first moment they met.

A couple of hours later, Magen awoke cold and stiff in Gabriel's arms, which still held her tightly across his chest. She lay there awhile, relishing the feel of his body against hers. Her heart swelled to see him sleep so peacefully. With a sadness in her heart she had never known the equal of, she pushed herself up and away from him. He stirred.

"I must go, Gabriel." He held on to her, but she resisted. "Please, Gabe."

"Don't go, Mae."

"It is you who are going, and go you must." The look of complete and utter loss in Gabriel's face wrenched her heart. "I will be here," she promised, looking at him now from the light cast from the door she had pushed opened—"waiting for you," she whispered.

Tears flooding her eyes, Magen made her way back to the house in the cold dark of the winter night.

Chapter 25

Losses and Gains

When Magen awoke in her own bed late the next morning, she lay there quietly. She was alone in the house; she felt it, just like she somehow knew Gabriel had already left. She felt his absence. It felt like part of her heart had been sheared away. She forced herself to get up and get dressed. Her body felt heavy, cold. But in spite of the loss she felt, she could not help but be aware of another feeling, something like awe.

She had never felt this way about another person. It was as if all her life she had been waiting for something she didn't even know existed. Other people must have felt these feelings before—surely she and Gabriel did not invent them, she thought smiling to herself. Yet she had never witnessed this kind of love between two people. She had not seen it between her father and Sara, nor between anyone she could ever remember. She knew Eliza and Avery loved one another, but in a different way.

Magen made her way downstairs to the kitchen. She was grateful to see the pot of steaming hot coffee hanging on the hearth's hook, and she poured herself a cup of the strong liquid. She donned her woolen scarf and mittens, and braced herself for the cold. Outside she felt a sense of quiet envelop her. She had no idea when she and Gabriel would manage to be together again, but for the first time in her life, Magen felt whole. She no longer felt like that little girl, watching down the road, hoping she'd see her Pa at last making his way back home. The pledge she and Gabe had made to one another last night had changed everything. And she believed in it.

Aunt Eliza opened the front door just as Magen was coming out. She asked Magen if she had had any breakfast.

"No," Magen answered, "I wasn't hungry."

The two of them walked out into the cold bright sunshine.

"Gabriel left at first light," Eliza said.

"Yes. I know."

Looking at Eliza, Magen wanted to share her happiness with her—and her sadness. She wanted to find the words to describe the joy she and Gabriel experienced last night, but she feared her words would sound foolish. She couldn't bare to diminish what they had experienced, so she remained silent. She took her aunt by the hand and said, "I've been blessed to find both you and Gabriel, Aunt." Then she kissed Eliza on the cheek.

Eliza, taken aback, seemed pleased. "With Gabriel gone, your workload will increase, Magen. I hope you'll be as grateful to be here in February when we're waist deep in snow." With that, they got on with the day's work.

Weeks passed. December came and went, and the three of them—Eliza, Avery, and Magen—welcomed in the new year of 1816 sitting in front of the kitchen fire after a long day of relentless work with the herd. They had drunk a toast—Eliza and Magen drinking a bit of the "old orchard," while Avery drank the light cider. That, and a foot and a half of new snow, was the only thing that marked an otherwise normal day. January's bleakness and cold began to get to Magen. The days were hard and she lacked her usual energy. More and more, Magen kept to herself, which worried Eliza and Avery. Eliza began to insist that Magen help Jane out in the house more. She thought the strenuous field work was taking a toll on Magen's health.

Icy January days did indeed turn into frigid February ones. But Magen was no stranger to bitter cold. Her mood began to gradually lift. February's snows were deep and quiet. She felt a stillness take hold deep inside herself. A welcomed peace came over her. Eliza and Avery were relieved. She waited for word from Gabriel, but heard nothing.

Magen found she liked having more time to herself indoors. She had always enjoyed cooking, but Sara had never encouraged her. She would first see to Jane and Emmy's work and then give herself over to the solitary tactile efforts of chopping spices, kneading dough, and preparing stew in front of the crackling fire in the hearth. The fragrances and the heat that came from her kitchen each evening nurtured her.

Whenever Eliza began to fret over Magen, Avery would chide her, "Let the lass alone. Everyone deserves a bit of solitude."

One evening after eating a meal served especially for Avery—rump of beef served with bannock bread, potatoes, and peas cooked in broth—Eliza, sitting by the fire resting her feet in a pan of hot water, said that she had heard from Louise Reynolds that Gabriel Thayer had been spotted over in Tucker Gorge making a purchase of a horse.

Avery, who had sat listening, said, "Is there more to this fascinating tale?"

"No, no. Just thought Magen might want to know, is all."

"And so she knows," Avery said. He lit his pipe, puffed, and bellowed out clouds of gray smoke.

Truth be told, hearing Gabriel's name brought up out of the blue like that gave Magen a jolt. She became so uneasy that she excused herself from the table and retired to her bedroom for the evening.

Avery stood like a gentlemen to let her pass and flashed Eliza a vexed look.

As Magen disappeared above the stairs, he said, "Why did you mention the lad's name like that, Eliza?"

"I don't know. I think I just wanted to see how she would react."

Looking at her for a bit, Avery said, "Ach! the girl is just tired. I'll be heading off to bed myself here shortly, and so should you, lass."

Upstairs, Magen pulled on her warm woolen nightdress and quickly climbed under her quilt. She lay there shivering. *Why was Gabriel buying a horse in Tucker Gorge?*, she wondered. *It wasn't so very far away that he couldn't have paid Creed Farm a visit during his trip, or gotten word to her to meet him halfway.* One moment she felt exhilaration at the memory of her night with Gabriel, and the next moment she was on the verge of tears, realizing that she hadn't heard from him since then. *How could he possibly go for so long without a word?*

In addition to missing Gabe, Magen had started to feel physically unwell. She had trouble being around food sometimes. She didn't want to worry Eliza, but lately she slept as if she had been drugged and found it difficult to get up in the morning. She dreaded that first shock of the cold floor on her feet and the icy water in her chamber basin. And for the first time ever, Magen, on occasion, was huffy and short-tempered toward both Avery and Eliza. At times, she even showed irritation with the animals she worked with. Eliza grew more concerned and watchful as the days passed.

Cold February days plodded on into arctic-cold March days. Judging by the short outbursts of temper and irritation at Creed Farm, the winter cold was getting the better of them all. On a dark mid-March afternoon, when deep snow had slowed the activities of the farm, Eliza, Avery, and Magen were sitting in the kitchen in front of the blazing hearth discussing one of the rams' health problems. In order to conserve heat, the kitchen was the only room in the house now being used regularly. Magen slept on an old cot next to the hearth rather than go up to her frigid room and light the small fire there. When Jane and Emmy stayed overnight, they slept in the hallway off of the pantry downstairs. Avery maintained a bed in one of the small outbuildings, as did any field hand who was bunking at the farm. A blazing fire in a half-chopped barrel kept that warm.

After a thorough discussion around the table of how to treat the ram, they all jumped to hear heavy-booted feet on the front porch. Before Avery could get to the door, it opened. Young William Hart and his brothers Peter and Joe, lads who had been shepherding at Creed Farm since the wolf attacks last summer, burst noisily into the kitchen, all talking at once.

Avery raised both hands to quiet them down, and asked William to tell the tale.

"It's either a rustler or a sheep killer, Mr. Mackay. East meadow. We went to check it out but got there too late. Two ewes are down, but we can't make out what's happened."

Eliza and Avery had their coats and hats on before they even sat down to pull up their boots. Eliza instructed Magen to prepare bandages for their return just in case there were injuries. Off they went in a swirl of snow, as Magen watched them from the front kitchen window. She knew that either scenario, rustler or predator, could be bad news—especially this time of year, when the snow made it difficult to protect the sheep. She paced around the kitchen, fretting.

Long after midnight, Magen stirred from a fitful sleep in her chair by the kitchen fire. Eliza came in first, followed by Avery and the Hart boys. Magen saw that Peter's coatsleeve was torn, and that there was blood on all the Harts' jackets.

"Get hot water and bandages, Magen, and the medicines from my bag," Eliza said hurriedly. She ushering the men over to the fire. All three Hart brothers sat down dazed at the long trestle table, waiting to be ministered to.

"What was it, Avery?" Magen asked.

"Our pack of wolves is back, Magen, starving and vicious. I killed at least one, and William wounded another. But they'll be back."

"It didn't attack you, surely?"

"No, but young Pete got clipped in the crossfire."

"It was my own fault. I was behind the herd and took some buckshot in my arm," Peter offered.

"Let me see your arm, then," Magen said, insisting that Eliza sit as well. As she cleaned the wound on the boy's arm, he was drained of all color and looked exhausted. "You look as though you've all been savaged," Magen said inspecting the others.

"No, Miss. This here is sheep's blood on us. We tried to save them, but they were too far gone," William said.

"Tomorrow we'll have to move the entire herd into the fenced yard," Avery said. "I don't know how they're all going to fare in so small an area, but we have no choice. At least they'll be more protected. We can keep a better eye on them there."

Brushing wisps of hair from her face in that impatient way that she had, Eliza said, "The wolves are hungry, the snow-cover is deep and early this year. They'll try again."

"Not tonight they won't," Avery said with assurance. "They'll move on, head further east. We'll have to warn the Reynolds' to be on the lookout. I'll send a messenger. The boys can bed down in my shed tonight. Magen, I'll bring back their shirts—perhaps you can soak them in the kettle tonight."

"I guess that's about all we can do for now, Avery," Eliza said.

As she spoke, off in the distance, the howling of a lone wolf stopped them cold. The menacing sound soon was joined by another, then another, until a chorus of the unearthly cries echoed through the hills.

"They know they've lost one of their own," Avery said.

"I'm that grateful we didn't lose one of *our* own this night," Eliza said. "I thank you all for what you did. It seems we're always at war these days. If it's not the Brits, it's nature itself, is it not?"

Chapter 26
The Allerdice Remedy

Young Peter's arm looked better in the light of day. It was a superficial wound that would heal sooner than the memories of the wolf attack. Days later, Aunt Eliza and Avery discussed new reports of sheep savaging in Saint Rock. Their faces were grim.

As Magen served more hot tea, Eliza stood up and said with a forced cheerfulness, "I have an announcement. We've been working hard and worrying ourselves sick; it's time we had an afternoon out. As luck would have it, we've been issued an invitation for just such an affair!"

Both Avery and Magen looked at Eliza with surprise. "An invitation? From whom?" Avery wanted to know. Eliza informed them that they would be attending an anniversary frolic.

"Ach! Not the Allerdice affair, Eliza!"

Magen, who'd never heard the term "anniversary frolic," didn't know how to react.

"To pile on the agonies of winter," Avery started to explain, "every March, the family Allerdice insists that every able-bodied Vermonter, as if they have nothing better to do, attend their *frolic*," he grumbled. "Only Lady Allerdice could come up with a name such as that."

"Avery, come now. They offer generous tables of food and drink. Neighbors come from miles around to attend."

"They come to eat, not frolic! And I know for a fact you have been invited to this event every year, Eliza Creed, but I have never known you to attend!"

Eliza responded with a steely gaze. "The truth is, I think we could all do with a bit of cheer this year." Then, looking straight at Magen, she added, "Wouldn't it be nice to spend some time with people your own age for a change, Magen?"

Magen couldn't have been more surprised by Eliza's question.

"Why, Aunt Eliza, I never considered it. But if you wish to attend, I'll gladly accompany you. I've never attended an *anniversary frolic* before. Besides, all that food sounds a little tempting. Doesn't it Avery?"

"Oh, no you don't, lass. You'll not be getting me over to that woman's house! She tries to railroad every unmarried male into dancing with that daughter of hers."

"Now Avery, don't be unkind," Eliza said.

"I hold nothing but the deepest sympathy for young Lucinda Allerdice. With a mother like that, the girl has no hope of happiness. But I'll not put myself through that ordeal again. I went once, years ago. That was enough for a lifetime."

"It sounds like Miss Wordleave's First of the Year social in Sackitt's Ridge," Magen explained with a laugh. "Sara wouldn't miss it for anything, but Pa always had a ready excuse for being somewhere else."

"See there?" Avery raised an eyebrow toward Eliza, "I'll be more than happy to deliver you two fine ladies to this affair in our very own sleigh. But attending the event myself, I cannot do. Not even for you, Eliza."

"The invitation was made to all of us, Avery."

"And I anxiously look forward to an extended account of the festivities." With that, Avery tipped his hat and made his way back to the bunk house, leaving clouds of smoke in his wake.

"The old coward!" Eliza said, trying to sound stern but knowing she would not change Avery's mind about attending.

The next morning came soon enough. Eliza and Magen raced through their chores. Both of them felt peculiar trading their work wardrobes in for dress-up early in the day. Magen didn't mind as much as Eliza. But instead of grumbling, Eliza looked resigned, "I guess I shouldn't lose all sight of the fact that I am in fact a female. Right, Magen?"

"Aunt Eliza, that is the first time I have ever heard you admit to this unalterable failing," she teased sarcastically. Although Magen wouldn't say it outloud, she would much rather have gone back up to her warm featherbed with a large mug of hot tea for a nap. But she didn't want to seem ungrateful for the invitation to join Eliza, so she tried to act excited. Maybe she could make a friend or two her own age, and there was always the possibility that a charming stranger would sweep Aunt Eliza off of her feet.

It was well past three o'clock when Magen and Eliza left the warmth of the house to see Avery sitting in the sleigh outside with a broad grin plastered across his face. Determined not to let him see her discomfort, Eliza assumed the demeanor of a well-placed socialite on her way to an outing and waited for his assistance in to the sleigh. Overplaying the part of the royal escort, Avery delicately handed them both up into the sleigh.

"Just drive, please, Avery," Eliza said in a dry tone, stopping the shenanigans.

Grinning still, Avery flicked the reins, and the ringing of the harness bells spurred Pinetop and Betsy into a brisk canter. They pulled the graceful sleigh down the snowy path, where hemlock and spruce bowed their snow-laden branches in respect to the grand travelers.

A sleigh ride on a good snow-packed trail was a wonderful change from the bone-jarring movement of a wagon ride on a rutted dirt road. Magen loved gliding along, with the piercing blue sky and bracing wind in her face. It reminded her of a long patch of meadow near the cabin in Sackitt's Ridge that their Pa would take her to with Carrie when the snow was good and deep. Their sleigh had been much smaller than this one and was pulled only by Pinetop, but on those rare outings with her Pa, Magen would close her eyes and imagine that she flew through a starlit sky. Carrie would squeal in delighted terror, but Magen never made a sound. She closed her eyes now and felt that fragile connection to the child she once had been.

"I'll be back in a couple of hours for you," Avery said as he pulled the sleigh to a gradual stop.

Magen wished the journey had taken longer. But she threw off the woolen blanket and pulled herself out as Avery assisted Eliza. With a wink and a nod from Avery, they headed inside.

They entered the two-story Dutch colonial house in the middle of Saint Rock village, and Magen was impressed by the number of people standing around the ornately furnished parlor. Candles and whale-oil lamps burned brightly from wall sconces and tabletops. Panoramic landscapes and scenes from the Revolution were painted on the richly textured wallpaper of the front entranceway. In the back sittingroom, where the walls were painted a Chinese red, the furniture had been removed for dancing. The crowd, however, was rather somber. Magen noticed the few Windsor chairs lining one wall had been claimed already by the elderly guests who were more intent on eating than socializing. A smaller connecting hallway held a large oak table laden with every food one could imagine. An overstuffed roast pig graced one end of the table while a large braised hen was placed on the other. Smaller side tables displayed rows of pumpkin, mince, and fruit pies, teacakes and sweetened dough balls, little pastries filled with meat, plum pudding, and three kinds of root vegetables in sauce. To top off the elaborate spread were two large punch bowls, one filled with eggnog and the other with a drink called Flip—a mixture of rum, beer, and sugar. The more potent mixture was by far the more popular.

The male guests easily outnumbered the female guests at this bowl. Bits and pieces of conversation Magen picked up concerned the weather, end-of-war politics, and whatever was to be done about the wolf pack menacing the local herds.

The Allerdices were clearly no strangers to entertaining. Eliza had informed Magen on the way over that Mrs. Allerdice came from a refined Virginia family, and ever since arriving in the hills of Vermont, she believed it her Christian duty to bring high culture and the art of entertainment to the ignorant masses. The ulterior reason she entertained was to bag a suitable marriage partner for her one and only daughter, Lucinda.

As Magen was trying to adjust to the sheer abundance that surrounded her, Mrs. Allerdice charged toward her and Eliza.

"After all these years of ignoring my invitations, here you stand! The honor of your company and that of your niece has quite discombobulated me!" As Mrs. Allerdice's rather shaky high voice pronounced discombobulation, her three chins so keenly resembled the waddle of a turkey that Magen had to bow her head to keep from giggling. Regaining her composure, she made sure she didn't look at Eliza, certain they wouldn't be able to conceal their amusement. After that, Magen couldn't seem to take her eyes off Mrs. Allerdice's chins. She was short and round, and she had a head full of dark sausage curls that bounced in all directions whenever she spoke. And she spoke a lot. In fact, Magen realized, in a house filled with conversation, Mrs. Irene Allerdice's voice could be heard above all others.

She held her daughter, Lucinda, firmly by the arm and paraded her around the room, stopping in front of every eligible man. Lucinda, a plain girl, quite a few years older than Magen, had the same look as a frightened fisher cat Magen once surprised in the woods.

Lucinda was obviously trying her best to please. With a big toothy smile frozen across her face, she extended a trembling hand to every awkward, tongue-tied gentleman her mother foisted her upon. With every introduction, Mrs. Allerdice ticked off a list of Lucinda's accomplishments, even pointing out the girl's needlework samplers that hung framed over the mantle. After each gentleman attempted to respond with an appropriate compliment, Lucinda would offer up a wobbly little curtsy and be dragged off to the next fellow.

"Looks like all of nature is here, Magen," Eliza said under her breath as she stood sizing up the crowd and gesturing a hello here and there to those standing around the room. George and Louise Reynolds, both standing across the room next to the punchbowl looking uncomfortable in their Sunday best, came over and stood next to Eliza and Magen.

Mrs. Allerdice, with Lucinda in tow, eventually made her way back over to them, chattering away unceasingly.

"Ah Eliza, perhaps you should take the opportunity to introduce young Magen to the eligible men I've gathered here. You won't find a better selection anywhere else. That is why you brought your niece here, isn't it?"

"I just thought Magen might like a chance to meet some of the younger folks in the area. I do appreciate your invitation every year, Irene. And this year we were delighted that we could get away from the farm for an afternoon to join you and your family in your beautiful home," Eliza said. She sounded as though she had memorized the lines in her head and was relieved to get the short speech over with. "I think," she added, "that Magen has plenty of time and sense to find her own way into marriage. If, indeed, that's what she wants."

Lucinda and Magen, wide-eyed and mute, stood at attention, not daring a response. Irene decided to change tactics. Looking straight at Magen, she said to Eliza, "Sorry to hear about the loss of your barn, dear. We heard young Gabriel Thayer stayed up at your place and helped Avery rebuild it. But then we heard he left."

Before Magen had a chance to say anything, Eliza responded, "Young Mr. Thayer is a fine carpenter, Irene. We did hire his services after I lost my barn. Unfortunately his mother took ill, not long after his father passed. So Gabriel has returned to Bellingham to assist her."

"You must miss him terribly," Irene's curls bobbed on either side of her chubby face as she tried to console Magen.

But again Eliza was quicker. "Yes, he's a fine lad, young Thayer. Avery and Magen and I do miss his help around the farm. But he may be back. We'll just have to wait and see how it goes for the Thayer family. They have certainly had their trials," she finished. Then putting her hand on Magen's she said, "I've been telling Magen what a wonderful cook you are, Irene, we must go and sample the marvelous things you and Lucinda have prepared for your guests."

Hoping she had gotten the last word, Eliza steered Magen away from Irene and, followed by the Reynolds, made their escape into the next room.

Magen helped herself to a dainty plate of smoked meat and petit fours. She nodded and smiled at the people she had met once or twice before in town, and then pretended to be unaware of the curious stares of the others.

But if Magen felt on display here, so too, she thought, was Eliza. As the tedious afternoon wore on, Magen observed Aunt Eliza gracefully fend off suitor after improbable suitor. Like in town that day, everyone stopped to try and get a word in with Eliza Creed. But George and Louise Reynolds were the only ones she engaged in conversation. Eliza Creed kept herself to herself, Magen remembered Gabe saying once. Though this didn't prevent people from trying to talk to her; everyone seemed anxious to seize the rare opportunity to socialize with this enigma of a woman. While Eliza never gave any encouragement, she also was never unkind, Magen noticed. No one ever felt the least bit rejected as she smiled and moved past them, inquiring after their health and families.

Magen couldn't help but feel proud of her aunt. The way she carried herself reminded Magen of her Pa. She had always liked the fact that he too had never acted as if he noticed the attention other women paid him.

Magen had gone to some pains with her own appearance today. She had pulled her long black shiny hair back in a french-knot against her neck and worn her best dress, a form-fitting but plain woolen gown, in a light blue that set off her golden skin. She felt empathetic toward Lucinda Allerdice, and complimented her on her fine dress. Lucinda looked down at herself as if surprised to see that she indeed was wearing a fine dress. Then she turned her wide-eyed gaze toward Magen, like a mystic reading the oracles. Magen began to feel uncomfortable and couldn't think of how to keep the conversation going. She began to feel close and hot and uncomfortable.

"I'm afraid I'm feeling a bit...well, that is, I think I need some air," Magen freed herself and started to make her way toward Eliza across the room, but Eliza was deep in conversation with Louise Reynolds. So instead, she made her way down the back hall, grabbed her cloak and flew out the back kitchen door. As soon as the cold air hit her face, a wave of nausea doubled her over. After a few minutes, the door opened again behind her. This time it was a worried Eliza attempting to sneak out unnoticed. She saw Magen right away and brushed back the hair from Magen's pale face.

"What is it, Magen? Are you sick?"

"Oh Aunt, how long will it be before Avery comes for us? I feel I must return home to bed. Something is amiss. Perhaps it was the sweets and rich food."

"Let's walk out front. He may be here now," Eliza said, taking Magen's cloak and wrapping it around her shoulders.

Much to their relief, Avery was waiting in the sleigh. As he spotted Magen's pasty complexion, concern registered on Avery's face as well. Eliza shot him a look of some alarm, and he knew not to delay with questions. He helped them both into the sleigh. Magen was relieved Eliza asked her no more questions. What she had suspected for some time, now she knew was true. She was pregnant with Gabriel's child. She just didn't know how to tell Aunt Eliza.

Later that night, Eliza and Avery sat at the kitchen table together. Magen had retired early to her bed after eating nothing more than a bowl of broth and a little bread. After a long silence that Avery knew better than to intrude on, Eliza said, "I believe we need to go and visit our young friend in Bellingham."

"We should go see Gabriel, you mean?" Avery asked.

"I do."

"What is it, lass?" Avery asked.

"The reason is upstairs laying in her bed."

"Do you think taking her to him, you can set in motion some kind of remedy for the melancholy that has taken over our girl, Eliza?"

"I think it's more than melancholy that affects our Magen. And I think young Gabriel should know about it as well."

A slow comprehension reached Avery's eyes as he realized Magen must be with child.

"To watch Magen go through this alone is heartbreaking. I won't stand for it. If there's something I can do to prevent that, I will."

"She's not alone, Eliza. Magen has us."

Chapter 27

A Visit to Bellingham

The next dawn broke too soon for Magen. Curled up tight in a ball in her warm bed, she couldn't bear to face another cold March day. But face it she must. She knew things had changed for her. In fact, she had known for some time that nothing would ever be the same again. She forced herself up as she had been doing for weeks, dressed herself in layers for warmth, and headed downstairs.

Eliza was up and waiting for her. "Feeling better, Magen?" she asked, with concern etched in her face.

"Yes, Aunt, I am. Though, I confess, I can't seem to find my strength these days. Forgive me for being a lay-about. You're shorthanded as it is."

"Don't concern yourself over the farm, Magen. There are hired hands capable enough to handle the farm for a few days without us."

"Another outing, Aunt?" Magen asked in alarm.

Eliza held back a smile. "Not as such, Magen. Avery and I need to make a trip to Bellingham to see a farmer there about a small herd. You could come along and pay Gabe a visit. What do you say?"

Magen was caught off-guard. It was like Eliza could read her mind. "Why, Aunt! I had not even considered such a trip," she fibbed. "You don't think it would be too brash a thing for me to go and see him?"

"Nonsense, child. I've never held with pretensions. Bonds between friends can be lost if one isn't careful. Besides, it wouldn't make sense for us to have business in Bellingham and not look in on him."

Magen held back tears, but couldn't hold back her relief. She put her arms around Eliza and hugged her hard. "Thank you," was all she could manage to say.

"I thought taking you to the Allerdices and introducing you to some young people would help improve your spirits. I see now, it wasn't one of my best ideas. Go and put some warm things together and I'll see to Jane and Emmy while Avery prepares the sleigh. We can be there by tomorrow evening," Eliza said, addressing Magen's back as she ascended the stairs with more energy than she had felt in days.

All the way to Bellingham Magen had to keep her emotions in check. The thought of seeing Gabe again made her giddy. The first day of the journey was long and uncomfortable; newly fallen snow slowed their progress, and the terrain was sometimes steep. Magen and Eliza huddled close together in the back seat of the sleigh snuggled under woolen blankets. They were grateful for the hot bricks Emmy had included to keep their feet warm.

Avery took the brunt of the raw wind as he sat in front driving the team of two horses hard through the brisk March wind. Much like February, March had seen long stretches of considerable snowfall. Today the sun shone dully like a smudge in the gray winter sky, with very little warmth to share. After tramping through the woods for six hours or more, the horses had had enough.

The weary travelers pulled into the tiny village of Antrim Corners at about seven that evening. They had been hearing wolves howling off in the distance all day, and Magen knew they were all wondering about the wisdom of leaving hired hands in charge of the farm. Wolf and panther attacks on helpless herds had become a common complaint throughout the region. "With the heavy snow cover, the beasts are hungry," Avery put it in his usual succinct way.

Avery knew the proprietor of a local tavern in town and could vouch for its safety as well as its hot food. They stopped there, and the three were ushered into a long dining hall where pine tables lined the south wall. A couple of other weary travelers sat at one, and Magen, Eliza, and Avery chose another close to the fire. It wasn't long before the proprietor himself brought them three hearty bowls of stew. "Mister Mackay, it's been a while since we've had the pleasure of serving you. Welcome back."

"Aye, we're pleased to take advantage of your fine fare, Edward. How have you been keeping?"

"Ah, times have been better. I'll just have our young lad see to your horses, and I'll show you to your rooms after you've had a chance to eat."

They devoured their stew and coffees, and Avery was then shown to a room at the top of the stairs, which he would share with two other men traveling west. Magen and Eliza were shown to a back room on the first floor, which they shared with the wife of one of the upstairs travelers.

"If we were to ever face any real danger," Eliza reassured Magen, "I have this," she said, pointing discreetly to a long, slender dagger strapped onto her leg underneath her woolen stocking. "I have never once needed to use it, but it has always helped my confidence."

Magen smiled to herself. She was surprised to learn that Eliza's confidence ever flagged.

They all slept hard and were off at first light after a breakfast of tea and buckwheat cakes. Magen knew the Thayers' home was situated in the middle of the town of Bellingham.

"The rumors that circulate," Avery said once they'd resumed their journey, "are that Gabriel's mother, Petra, in spite of her own health problems and having problems with her eyesight, tried to maintain a lofty lifestyle long after her family's Boston investments dried up. Living life on a schoolteacher's salary was never part of her or her daughter's plans. Gabriel's father, Eben, was a decorated soldier of the Revolution, but lost his chance at earning a fortune when he lost the use of his legs. It was not a happy marriage by all accounts."

"Let's not indulge in gossip, Avery," Eliza chided. Then she added, "I wonder if Gabriel's mother really will return to the Boston area now. After all, they've lived in Bellingham for a good many years now."

Magen listened to their speculation and worried. How free had Gabriel been to pledge himself to her? Would he see her visit as more trouble for himself? *The last thing he may want now is a reminder of another obligation.* The closer they got to Bellingham, the more anxious she became. Perhaps Eliza was right, though. Maybe she should be bold where Gabriel was concerned. They had, after all, pledged themselves to one another. *Didn't it follow then, that they were both responsible for whatever had resulted from their night together?*

The horses made good time and they pulled into Bellingham around four o'clock. Again Avery's worldliness served them well, for he knew which inn in Bellingham was the most respectable and served the least objectionable food.

The Hotel Bellingham was situated in the center of town, not far from the Thayer home. As Avery helped Eliza and Magen climb down from the sleigh, he said he would go in and see about the sleeping accommodations for them and the horses, and Eliza should inquire about the possibility of a meal.

Eliza and Magen were shown over to a pair of brace-backed Windsor chairs in front of a roaring fire by the wife of the innkeeper. She assured them that she would prepare a table for three while they sat and warmed themselves. After a bit they were shown to a table by a young man employed by the hotel.

Eliza turned to him and said, "I wonder if you could get a message to a Mr. Gabriel Thayer that we would like to see him. I believe his family's home is close by." Eliza looked over at Magen who was avoiding the eyes of the young man now looking conspicuously at her. "Mr. Thayer has done carpentry work at my farm," Eliza continued, "and I wish to discuss some business with him."

The young man assured them that he would send word to the Thayer residence immediately. As Avery entered the room and joined them at the table, both women relaxed.

"I don't know why I'm explaining myself to that boy. It's no one's business but our own," Eliza said to Magen under her breath. Magen lowered her eyes as she tried to smile at Eliza, but she too was nervous.

"I believe you put forth just the right tone, Aunt Eliza."

Avery motioned over the proprietor's wife and ordered supper plates for them all.

Heavy earthenware crocks of steaming pork stew were brought to their table and a pot of strong black tea made them all forget for a moment the discomforts of travel. The proprietess, Mrs. Beecher, fussed around their table, offering yet another helping of this or that. Noticing the slight exasperation in Eliza's face, the woman went to great pains to explain that her best serving dishes had been left out on the tables overnight by her "less-than-helpful son." Many of her pieces had broken or cracked from the cold.

"But I can still offer my guests hot bread straight from the spider skillet if you wouldn't be offended at such an undignified presentation."

Eliza assured her that no crockery was safe in a New England house in winter, and that they had humble requirements. Mrs. Beecher, relieved and pleased, added a few extra cubes of sugar to their tea. Afterwards, they heard the woman flutter back to her kitchen where she gave her son another dressing down for being so forgetful.

Chapter 28

The Meeting

"Sara always said it was impossible to get a decent meal outside one's own home. But I think she may have been mistaken," Magen said after polishing off a good part of her stew within the first quarter of an hour.

"So you're feeling less peckish?" Eliza asked.

Magen nodded and smiled with a sigh of contentment. Then they were distracted by something happening at the front of the dining room. Magen turned to look and saw Gabriel standing there, hat in hand, staring at her with a look of genuine surprise and what she hoped was happiness. As he walked over to their table, his eyes did not leave Magen's.

"They told me you were here. I thought at first it was a hoax. I prayed it wasn't," he said, and pulled a chair up to their table.

"Don't mind us now, lad," Avery said with a grin toward Eliza. Gabriel made a cursory nod toward them, and then took Magen's hands in both of his. "How goes it with you, Mae? It is so good to look on your face."

Magen felt like a tight knot inside her had just loosened. She let out a long sigh and stared at him. Tears threatened at the back of her eyes, because she was so relieved to be looking into his again. But she also remembered how he had not contacted her when he was so close to Creed Farm, and she pulled back slightly.

Trying not to let the hurt sound in her voice, she said, "We are so pleased to see you, Gabriel. Avery and Eliza have business here. And I thought it would give me the chance to look in on you. I haven't heard from you in so long, we wondered about your circumstances. How does your family fare?"

Taken slightly aback by her formal manner, Gabriel tried to recover his demeanor. He sat up straighter in the chair, lowered his hands and for the first time looked at Eliza and Avery.

"I see, business. Yes, yes, of course. Well, my mother is not well—in mind or body. Her condition is deteriorating, and while she is aware of it, she refuses to accept it. My sister and I try to do her bidding. You would have to know my mother to understand how monumental a task that is."

"You'll be glad to know the work on the second loft in the barn is a good addition and is holding up well, lad. A good suggestion it was. I couldn't have done it without your hard work," Avery said.

"Good. Good. I had hoped I could help you finish that addition. But I'm glad it's done and meets with your approval, Avery."

"It was a relief to me and the animals to have it completed before the heavy snows came," Eliza added.

Looking from Magen to Gabriel and back to Magen, Eliza continued, "We're here to see about a herd, Gabriel. I wonder if Avery and I could impose upon you to entertain Magen while we see to our business tomorrow?"

Eliza could see Magen's demeanor lighten at the suggestion.

"We are much too tired after our long trip, and I'm sure your mother needs you at home this evening. But in the morning if you could come for Magen, Avery and I will not be long at our task," Eliza said.

"I would be more than happy to spend time with Magen tomorrow, Miss Creed … if she agrees," Gabriel replied, searching Magen's face for encouragement.

"Very good," Eliza responded, not waiting for Magen to reply.

"Are you sure you can spare the time from your work, Gabriel?" Magen asked, still feeling slightly wounded that Gabriel had not been in touch all of this time.

"Of course I'm sure, Magen. How would it be if I came by in the morning for you about seven?"

"Let's make it eight," Magen replied, and she stood up from the table.

Gabriel got up then, too, and knocked over the chair behind him. He caught it before it fell to the floor. Blushing furiously he said, "I will look forward to tomorrow then. Goodnight." Magen and Eliza were already halfway to the stairs.

"That worked out well now, didn't it, lad?" Avery said, grinning up at Gabe.

"If you say so," Gabriel mumbled as he walked slowly to the door and left.

In the night, Eliza woke to the sound of Magen throwing up in the chamber basin. She went over to Magen and mopped her brow with a damp cloth.

"I see you are again experiencing a sick stomach?" Eliza asked in a sympathetic tone.

"I don't travel so well, Aunt. I confess. I'm sorry to wake you."

"You have done well, child. Gone quite a bit further under your own esteem, I'd say, than most girls your age."

"Aunt Eliza, I fear I am with child," Magen blurted out before she could stop and think.

"I believe you are right," Eliza said, cupping Magen's chin in her hand. "It's not the end of the world you know. Things like this never are." She smiled. "Why don't you try and get a good night's sleep before you talk to Gabriel tomorrow? Hush, now."

Magen's relief that her secret was out was so great that she fell deeply asleep within minutes.

Gabriel was waiting downstairs when she came down at eight sharp. She had managed to eat a bit of the bread and milk that Eliza brought up to her before she and Avery had taken off to tend to their business. Magen wondered where exactly they were headed, but they were out the door before she had a chance to ask.

Magen had on her best gray dress with white lace cuffs and neckline, and her long cape. She hoped her attire made her look somewhat sophisticated, because at the moment she felt unsure of herself. Gabriel had been standing in the lobby waiting for her when she made her way self-consciously down the stairs. He complimented the way she looked, but when he went to take her hand she held it back. Seeing his look of hurt, she smiled and said, "We should be off now, don't you think?" To Magen's surprise, Gabriel had a horse and buggy out front.

"There's a place I like to go that I think you would like to see, Magen. Do you mind?"

"No. Of course I don't mind."

She did take his hand then as he helped her up into the buggy. He held onto it a bit longer than necessary. As the two rode away in the carriage, Eliza and Avery watched with interest from the window of Claussen's General Store across the street.

The sun was shining on the buggy, but the cold March air bit at their faces. Gabriel had placed a wool riding blanket over Magen's lap before leaving town, and now he tucked it in closer to her and checked that her collar was up to shield her face from the raw wind. As the buggy left the village, the stares from the people of Bellingham drifted out of sight. Magen began to feel less self-conscious now that they were alone. In fact, she felt warm and happy sitting next to Gabriel again. They rode for quite a while alongside a frozen-looking river. Large snow-covered rocks broke the flow of the water and ice. Gabriel pulled the horse over to the right with a *whoa*.

"It's a short walk from here, Magen."

They made their way on a path that followed the river. Gabe led Magen by the hand. The two ducked their heads as they passed under thickets of bare sumac and gnarly grapevines that crowded the path; their way was canopied by huge oaks and evergreens. It felt to Magen as though they were walking through a frozen isolated arbor. It was beautiful. Gabe stopped at a clearing next to the river, so well hidden away she wondered how he ever came to find the place. Huge rocks stood like sleeping giants all around. The place was private and magical. Magen stood as close to the water as she could without getting her feet wet. She liked to see the river running just beneath the ice.

Gabriel, who had been standing back looking at her, came up beside her and took her by the arm. Before she knew what he was going to do he turned her toward him and kissed her hard.

Magen responded, but then pushed away from him.

"How could you not correspond with me all this time, Gabriel? It was like you forgot about me entirely!" Her angry words were out before she even knew she was saying them.

"Mae, I assure you, I didn't forget—not for a moment. I thought about writing you a letter. I started one many times. But all I could think to say was I love you, I need you, and I miss you."

"That would have done," Magen said, suddenly appeased. She inspected Gabriel's face. She saw the weariness around his eyes. The confusion she had been feeling herself soon turned to one of concern for him. "What is it, Gabriel? What aren't you telling me?"

"I don't want us together for only a day, Mae. Surely you know that!" he said angrily now. "When we made our pledge to one another it was for a lifetime together. Not stolen moments hidden from prying eyes."

Magen, relieved, went to him and this time took him by the arm turning his face to hers. "I have known this from the first, Gabriel. Doesn't that make us the most fortunate of two people? Why didn't you write the letter? I only needed reassurance."

"It's my obligations here. You know my father's last request was for me to look after Mother and Adele. I was the strong one, he said. They are not. It was the thing he knew I dreaded hearing the most, yet he asked me anyway."

Magen waited for what came next.

"Mother is losing her sight now," he continued. "I think she's terrified of ending up as helpless as she saw my father to be. She lashes out at me desperate for someone to take the blame for the unfairness of her life. We've employed nurse after nurse, but none will stay."

"And your sister? How goes it with her?"

"My mother has spent her small inheritance on my sister. Determined to make out of her what she herself once aspired to be—a lady of society," Gabe said with disdain. "Adele attended the finest finishing schools in the East. She has learned all about society and how to function in it, but nothing about earning her own keep."

"It's not easy for a woman," Magen said in Adele's defense. "Her options are limited."

"I have to help them find Adele a husband if I can, Mae. How else will she survive once Mother is gone?"

"I understand."

"I held my father in the highest esteem," Gabe continued miserably, as if Magen hadn't spoken. "He was kind and intelligent. Although he never complained of my mother's disposition, he did try and spare me from it. He was the one who insisted I leave when I was but a boy. My mother was furious. She didn't want me in the trades. She believed we were 'a cut above the rest of the rabble.'

"I earned my own wages, and I always sent money home. But I stayed away, leaving him to bear the brunt of their unhappiness. In the end, he asked me to return to take over. He must have believed I had it in me to do this," Gabriel said, sounding as though he was trying to convince himself once again.

"He had great faith in you," Magen said.

"My mother sits all day in a dark room waiting for blindness to overtake her, while Adele sits idle, barking orders at the hired girl. What is expected of me, I'm not sure. That's why I didn't write you, Mae," Gabriel explained as he paced back and forth like a caged animal.

Magen felt his frustration, but was unsure how to proceed.

"I have lived a long time on my own, as my own man. When I met you I believed I saw my future—our future. Now I can't see past the promise I made to my father. I can't ask you to leave a home you just found to take on this unhappy family."

"Have you told your mother about us?" Magen ventured.

"Yes. I told my mother and Adele about you the first night I returned. Mother went into a rage. Accused me of abandoning her as my father had done."

With tears in her eyes, Magen stood there numbly. The joy she felt earlier on first seeing him had turned to a sadness she couldn't bear. Regardless of his family's shortcomings, they needed him. He must stay. Magen knew, too, that he was right about her. She would be miserable if she were to leave Creed Farm and move in with Gabe's unhappy family. "Let's go back to town, now. This place grows colder by the minute."

Gabriel tried to take her hand, but she pushed him gently but firmly away and headed back down the path. When she looked into his eyes as they climbed into the buggy, she again saw that weariness. She knew that Gabe had been some months into this struggle with his mother and sister. How could she ask more of him now? She lowered her eyes from his searching ones, refusing to let him see her tears.

The trip back to the inn was cold and desolate but only took a few minutes—not enough time for Magen to compose her emotions. She didn't want to add to Gabriel's misery, so when he pulled the horse to a full stop and made to get out of the buggy, Magen slipped her hand into his.

"Don't get out, Gabriel. I can't bear saying goodbye to you again. Your father was right to believe in you. You do us both proud by living up to your promise to him. One day we'll live up to the promise we made to one another."

She couldn't think of what more she could say, yet she could not seem to take her hand away. Gabriel held on to it tightly.

"You are my family, Mae. I'll find a way to get back to you. I promise," he said, with a heat Magen could feel. They did not hug, nor did they kiss. Magen helped herself out of the buggy this time, and without another word she walked alone into the inn.

Magen's urgency to be gone was apparent to Eliza and Avery, who were waiting for her just inside in the foyer. She could see they were anxious for a report on her meeting with Gabriel. But it was not forthcoming. She didn't want to shut them out, but she found that she couldn't yet speak of what happened. The three of them decided to leave. More than anything, they needed Creed Farm. They returned to their rooms, packed, and met back in the lobby. Within the hour they were back in the sleigh and on their way home. Magen had never been so relieved or so heartbroken to leave a place.

Chapter 29

Home Again

The first part of the trip back was uncomfortable for Magen. She knew Eliza was curious about what had happened between her and Gabriel, but she still couldn't bring herself to talk about it. They stayed at the same tavern they had stayed at on their way down. Only this time Avery slept on the first floor, while Magen and Eliza took the smaller room at the top of the stairs. Theirs was a corn husk bed with a crank that had to be turned to tighten the ropes that held the mat of husks. It was an uncomfortable piece of furniture for two women to attempt to sleep in, and was made more so by the thumping of the headboard against the wall every time they turned over. Their one consolation was that they didn't have to share the room with a stranger.

After tossing and turning and trying to settle in, Eliza turned to Magen and brushed her hair away from her face. "It is, on occasion, acceptable to cry, Magen."

With this the tears began to flow. In great gasps they came, as if ripped from her body. All the love, fear and joy that Magen had been storing up inside came pouring out of her in waves. She cried for her dead sister Carrie, whose innocent young face she could no longer remember. She cried for women like Sara and Gabriel's mother, whose misery shut out any happiness around them. And she cried for her father and for her mother Ruth, who never got the chance to live out their dreams. After the tears for her family, Magen cried for herself and Gabriel—for their love that felt so tender and so raw she did not know how to protect it. Eliza held Magen and listened to the grief pour out of her. With all of her heart she wished she could take some of Magen's pain away, but all she could do was hold tight. Eventually, Magen fell asleep, exhausted.

The final day of their journey home was cold and blustery. Magen was quiet and withdrawn. Eliza exchanged glances with Avery, but neither pressed her for an explanation of her visit. After a long, cold and tiresome journey, the horses at last rounded the notch at Saint Rock, and were in a fair gallop by the time they reached the road to Creed Farm.

"I can't tell you how happy I am to be back at the farm, Aunt Eliza."

"And why not? It's your home," Eliza said, smiling.

Avery pulled the horses to a slow canter as they traveled up the oak-lined road to the house, and Eliza reached over and took Magen's hand.

"Don't ever forget that you are a Creed, Magen. And your child will be a Creed," she gripped Magen's hand. "You can never bring shame on us. We're family."

The relief she felt knowing that Eliza and Avery now knew the truth was as great for Magen as the relief she had felt the day Eliza told her she could stay at Creed Farm. She grabbed Eliza's firm grip with her other hand, pulled her close, and kissed her on the cheek. "I love you, Aunt Eliza."

The sleigh entered the stone pillars at the entrance to Creed Farm, and Avery turned to look at them. "What's with all the tears, lasses? Isn't it grand to be back home where we belong?"

Both women laughed as they looked with appreciation at the sheep in the barn yard, the rebuilt barn, and the house at the top of the hill with a ribbon of smoke dancing out of its chimney. Avery assisted them out of the sleigh, and they were all comforted to walk into a warm kitchen with a blazing fire in the hearth. Jane and Emmy greeted them with coffee on the boil. While Jane went out to assist Avery with the bags, Magen and Eliza settled into home.

The strong taste of chicory revived them both, but one look at Magen's exhausted face and Eliza insisted she retire for the evening. Grateful, Magen finished her drink and made her way up the stairs. Tonight she needed to be alone in her room, cold as it was, instead of sleeping in front of the hearth downstairs. No one questioned her. How comforting to not have to explain oneself, Magen thought, as she pulled off her traveling clothes and wrapped her grandmother's heavy, warm quilt around her weary body. She heard the howling of wolves off in the distance. Instead of feeling worried or desolate, Magen was surprised to feel a sense of calm at her core. Hearing the noises of the night creatures outside, she felt an incredible kinship with this house, with these ferocious winters, and with these uncommon people. No matter what happened between her and Gabriel, Magen knew she was home. She pulled the warm covers up to her frosty nose, and adjusted her woolen nightcap. It wasn't long before blissful sleep took over her exhausted body.

That night, Magen dreamed she was making her way across Fat Mountain once more. It was autumn, and Pinetop was having a difficult time pulling the large buckboard. She tried to help him up the stony path by pulling his lead rope, guiding him with care. She was frightened and worried at the steep drop-offs on either side of the wagon. Pinetop was skittish and uneasy. After she led the horse and wagon to level ground, Magen climbed to look inside the wagon.

There, a small group of people huddled together in a tight circle. At first she couldn't make out who they all were, but she soon recognized her father, Eliza, Gabriel, Avery, Jane, and Emmy. It looked as though they were shielding something or someone. Magen climbed in further and looked down to find a tiny baby wrapped in blankets. She picked the child up and reassured it and the huddle of protectors that all was well.

She awoke reluctantly to sleet and ice pelting the bedroom window. It was a blizzard outside, and she could see nothing but white. She lay still, listening to the eaves and timbers of the farmhouse creaking and groaning in the relentless northeast wind. She thought about her dream. It had left her with a feeling of peace and strength—a much welcomed feeling, considering the raucous storm just outside the walls of the house. But even more than that, she felt a sense of purpose begin to take shape. Her path seemed clear to her now, as she lay in that netherworld between sleep and wakefulness. Gabriel would have to find his own way back to her while living up to the promise he made to his father. Her purpose now was to treasure and protect the life that grew inside her and to help Eliza and Avery get the farm through the winter.

Snow covered the ground and disguised the familiar landscape outside her window. Magen heard Eliza downstairs before she pushed herself up to face the frigid house. A line of ice and snow had drifted in along her bedroom windowsill. The bed's brass warming pan had long grown cold. Magen could see her breath as she wrapped her woolen shawl around her shoulders. With teeth chattering, she donned her woolen stockings, breeches and shirt; she was more grateful than ever for the masculine clothes Jane had tailored to fit her. They kept her warm and hid her figure well. After shaking the ice crystals from her bed quilt, Magen straightened her room and made her way downstairs. She felt more resolute than she had in months, and she greeted Eliza with a smile.

"It looks as though that night's sleep agreed with you, Magen. It's good to see you smile," Eliza said. She fixed the kettle of water on its hook in the hearth.

"I know you've been worried about me," Magen began. "I would like to set your mind at ease."

"You told Gabriel how it is with you then? How did he respond?" Eliza asked with her usual directness.

"We love each other, Eliza. I think a part of me knew I loved him from the day we first met. We pledged ourselves to one another the night before he left. Our union didn't just occur in the heat of the moment." Magen explained, calmly resolute.

"I never supposed that it had. But that didn't quite answer my question. Does Gabriel know the outcome of your union?"

"He has family obligations," Magen continued in a strong but resigned tone of voice.

"Indeed he has—to you and yours!"

"His mother and sister have a hold on him now. He gave his father his word, you see, that he would take care of them after he died. He would not be the man that I esteem so well if he were to walk away from that promise before it's fulfilled."

"Did Gabriel ask you to stay, Magen? It is his home after all."

"I spent the first part of my life with Sara—a woman similar in nature to Gabriel's mother, from the way he describes her. She, too, felt the world had been unkind to her, and she needed to make those around her pay the price for it. I love Gabriel, but I will not spend my life in another unhappy home. More importantly, I will not allow my child to, either."

"So you never told Gabriel of the child you carry?" Eliza asked.

"Not yet, Eliza. It may have been wrong of me to withhold the information from him, but if I had told Gabriel he would have insisted that I stay. Please tell me that you meant it when you said Creed Farm will always be my home as well as my baby's."

Eliza stopped cold and gave Magen her full attention. Looking eye to eye, she took a deep breath as if she had just made up her mind about something.

"Sometimes the obstacles we face, Magen, may seem like our undoing. But, in fact, they may be the blessings we've waited for all of our lives. I trust your decision. I think it wise to let Gabriel have a chance to deal with his own family responsibilities before heaping more upon him. For now, I'll say no more about it. Come now, you've been carrying a load of worry by yourself for quite some time. Let Avery and I share some of the burden—and the joy. I was blessed the day you rode into my life. Soon we'll all be blessed with the presence of your child."

Magen listened, on the verge of crying.

"No more tears now, Magen. We don't have the time."

Chapter 30
Perspective

Magen was helping Avery out with the herd one morning, pleased as always to listen to his rambling monologue. "So far, 1816 has been brutal!" he said. "But New Englanders are accustomed to brutal. Now you must look for the subtle signs of spring, Magen, so as not to miss them."

Magen looked at Avery with a cocked eye.

"Come now, lass, tell me what you see." So Magen really looked. It didn't take long to notice the maple trees that lined the mountains blush ever so slightly with shades of scarlet, just here and there. The tamarack were beginning to take on their new wardrobe of golden needles, and the silver birch added just the right balance of bright to the tableau of muted colors. She smiled at Avery's grin.

"When the nights are cold enough and the days grow warmer, the sap in the maples will begin to run. Every year, we prepare for the running of the sap," Avery explained to Magen as they walked out to the barn together. "The season is late this year; some even wonder if we're going to have a sugaring time," he said in a worried voice, but then quickly lightened his tone. "But I want to make sure we'll be ready if conditions become right."

He had instructed the hired hands and Magen on how to tap the trees of the sugarbush on the hill by inserting sumac spiles or spouts into the inner bark to catch the sap that flowed like sweet water into the wooden buckets. Magen paid close attention. She had always wanted to make syrup, but Sara forbade any project that took time away from daily chores. Avery was delighted she wanted to help out. As was his way, he patiently explained to her how once the sap was collected in the wooden buckets it would be poured into the massive iron kettle, where it would be boiled down again and again over an outside fire to turn it into syrup, then brought into the kitchen for its final boiling down.

"All in all, it was a poor season last year," he said. "I hope we can make up for it this year. The syrup and maple sugar is the only thing we might have for trade come harvest time."

The sugaring process, Magen knew, was just a small part of this busy time of year. It also was the beginning of lambing season. Most sheep lambed in late spring, but their brand of Merinos lambed earlier. Eliza had taken on extra help as she always did at this time to keep up with the extra workload. She and Magen worked alongside the hired hands, frequently staying up until the wee hours administering to the ewes who had difficult births. If a ewe was unable to deliver on her own within an hour or so, they called in Avery. Magen had seen him time and again put right difficult breech presentations or lambs with their legs turned back. They also dealt with those reluctant ewes who had problems with their milk supply or wouldn't accept their young. This required hours of patient coaxing of the ewe and her lamb in a barnstall until the ewe would feed the lamb on her own. If this method didn't succeed, the baby lamb usually didn't survive unless it was hand-raised as a cosset.

With each new lamb that was brought forth, Magen felt a particular and personal thrill as she vigorously rubbed it with straw. She was feeling the new life growing within her, and there was nothing else to compare this feeling to. Every kick or flutter inside her belly gave Magen a deeply felt connection to the earth.

Even when they were up to their elbows in muck and work, Magen noticed Eliza and Avery keeping one eye on her, ensuring she didn't overdo. With her slender figure and the work clothes she wore it would be some time before her condition was obvious to others. Still, she thought Jane and Emmy must know already. Little got by Jane, and they were both being particularly attentive toward her. Since Eliza nor Avery ever wasted time worrying about what other people thought, Magen made a conscious decision not to indulge feelings of embarrassment either. As Eliza had said: there wasn't time.

After a long day in the fields trying to ensure the lambs were getting enough feed corn to survive the crucial first ten days of life, Magen hauled her tired body up to her room upstairs. Once again she wondered whether she should contact Gabriel and tell him the truth about her condition. It seemed that the further along her pregnancy progressed, the more she second-guessed herself. Still, she always came back to that final question— what good would it do to burden him with another responsibility just now?

Exhausted by the day's work, Magen changed into warmer, looser clothes and went back downstairs to fix a mug of tea. As she sat in the rocker in front of the kitchen window warming her cold hands on the mug, she noticed the dim light from the barn across the dooryard. She wondered what Eliza and Avery were so long about. Just as she was thinking how good her bed would feel to her this night, she realized that the closest she would ever get to being good was by making herself useful. So, with effort, she pushed herself out of the chair to see if she could help out.

She donned the woolen smock that hung by the door and made her way out to the barn. Sliding the heavy door open, she saw Eliza and Avery sitting on the floor cradling a haggard-looking ewe. The ewe had delivered twin lambs in a difficult birthing that had gone on too long. This was not just any ewe, but one of Eliza's favorite old dears—the one she called "The Queen."

Magen walked in and Eliza gave her a tired smile. "Come and see what the day has blessed us with," she said. Magen knelt down next to the two little lambs. As she rubbed them down with straw to warm them up, she said to Eliza, "This day has all but gone. Queenie has left it until the dark of night."

Avery had stopped cold. His arms were covered up to the elbows in blood and muck. "She's going to die, Eliza. Too much damage and infection here. The Queen's done in, lass."

Eliza looked startled at first. She inspected the sunken eyes in the old face of the ewe, and the tender, painful parts of her old body, and she nodded a reluctant agreement. "It's all so extraordinary, isn't it? To be alive and to know it with every fiber of your being? Still, we all have to know when to let go. The Queen has had her day. Magen and I will take the little ones to see if we can interest one of the other ewes into accepting them. Would you take care of this for me, Avery?"

Avery sat back on his haunches and nodded.

Eliza wrapped her arms around The Queen's large head one last time. "You've been a grand old dame for many long years. I'll miss you." With that, she heaved herself up with help from Magen, as if she too felt the coming of age in her bones. "The one life in payment for two. Nothing ever remains the same," Eliza said as she slowly left the barn.

Magen was reminded of something else Eliza had once said, "Creed Farm was all she knew of God. And all she needed to know."

Chapter 31

A Letter

Every day Avery read a story from the *New Hampshire Gazette* that he'd gotten in Saint Rock the week before, or he would relay a story he'd heard from a local farmer about what was going on in their area. All the news was the same: The effects of the unseasonable weather were getting harder and harder to deal with on farms in the Northeast. Heavy April rains soon turned into mud season. This year's winter had given way to a cold spring. Avery shook his head in disbelief as he put down the paper.

"We're certainly not the only ones dealing with this freakish weather," he grumbled. "Not that that makes it any easier."

After Avery had his say, Eliza noted a rider trying to make his way up the almost impassable road out front. "Between the snowmelt and rains, all wagons are unusable. But there's a rider out front trying to make it up the road on a single horse and even he's having a difficult time."

Magen rushed to look out the window and also saw the single horseman negotiating the ruts in the road toward the house. The rider was one of the sons of the Jarvis family Eliza knew from Tucker's Gorge.

Eliza went out to greet him. He was delivering a letter. The boy explained that the letter had been delivered some time ago, but since no one from the farm had been seen in town he took it upon himself to deliver it in person.

"Had to wait for a dry day, though, to make it through the mud slogs," he said, ending in a hopeful note.

Eliza thanked the boy and obliged him with two-pence for his trouble. Knowing at first glance who the letter was from, she took it back in to Magen.

"A letter for you, Magen."

Magen looked up from her sewing and turned to Eliza. "It must be from Gabriel."

"My thought as well."

Magen had never before received a letter, and her hands trembled a little as she inspected it. Eliza left the room to allow Magen some privacy. Magen wasted no time in unfolding the thin piece of parchment sealed at the edge.

My dearest Mae, she read. *I love you, I need you, and I miss you.*

Magen smiled remembering her and Gabe's conversation by the river.

I have no experience penning a letter, but I felt the need to do so now. There is no real news to share with you. At least nothing has happened here that would allow me to come to you.

Crestfallen, she read on.

My mother's eyesight is gone now. She has taken to her bed entirely. We've hired another nurse. So far she abides Adele's supervision. Adele waits on mother both day and night. I am the fortunate one to have my own work to do outside of this house.

I come home in the evening to a litany of complaints and demands—a house full of wretched people.

The carpentry work is plentiful though, and the men I work with are more experienced than I. Every day I learn new elements of my craft. In the evening I am much worn out from a long day's efforts. After seeing to mother, I fall into my bed readily enough and sleep like the dead until the sun rises and I get up and do it all again.

I know it is unworthy of a man to complain. My lot would not be so wretched if I didn't miss you so much. I worry you will lose all patience if I don't attempt to send you word of both my intentions and affections. Do not seek the affection of another. I tell myself our perseverance will be rewarded in the end.

Gabriel

Magen was heartened by the letter. Although it troubled her to hear the Thayer family so wretched, she was relieved to hear that he missed her and his affection for her remained constant. She was reassured that when Gabriel finally did come to her it would be on his own hook. Clearly his duty was there now; she could accept this.

Magen folded up Gabe's letter and put it in her apron pocket. Nothing had changed, yet the letter buoyed her spirits. She could write him back to reassure him, she thought. Yet if she did so, again omitting her condition, was that being dishonest with Gabriel? *Of course it was*, she had to admit.

But with each day that now passed, Magen felt more and more protective of the baby that grew inside her. She felt compelled to remain constant in her intentions toward her child and situation. She had perhaps learned a valuable truth in her short life, a truth that Gabe was also learning the hard way. *Right now is all one ever has.* Right now her responsibility was to their unborn child, and Gabriel's was to his mother. They were each where they should be. So she refrained from writing him or doing anything at all but what was in front of her to do.

Chapter 32

A Shadow Falls

Eliza and Avery commiserated every night after dinner over the effects the weather, including last fall's storm, was having on the farm's productivity. Every newspaper and pamphlet they could get their hands on despaired over a cold mud season that had lingered through most of May. Then, on May thirtieth, a widespread heavy frost hit. Not only was New England experiencing strange weather patterns, but frosts had hit as far south as Virginia, resulting in a late flowering season for much of the country.

When a heat wave hit in early June, everyone's spirits began to rise, only to be dashed again when a drastic drop in temperatures occurred a week later. Avery reiterated his theory that New Englanders simply accept brutal winters as their lot. But it was small consolation; brutal winters were only bearable because winter usually gave way to summer. Just not very clearly in this case. What could one think if one couldn't rely on nature to do its part? Magen saw the fear and worry in Eliza's and Avery's eyes.

One June morning, Avery left to go into town for supplies. Magen came downstairs earlier than usual. Seeing no sign of Eliza in the kitchen, she went out onto the front porch to see if she could spot her in the field. There was a funny feeling in the air, Magen thought to herself. Her skin felt prickly. *Was she just imagining this feeling of impending doom because of her condition?* She knew enough to realize that she was highly emotional these days, and her feelings couldn't always be trusted. She was aware lately how her heart would soar one moment only to plummet the next.

She stood looking out over the hills, and a slight breeze started to blow. Magen held her arms around herself, as she was wrapped in only a shawl and a loosely fitting cotton shift. Off in the distance, she saw Aunt Eliza making her way toward the house. Oddly, as Magen watched her slow progress, Eliza's far-off outline seemed to blur. Magen raised her hand, hoping to get her aunt's attention by waving. Eliza didn't see her, because she did not return the wave. Magen began to walk out to her. No sooner had she made progress over the first rise in the hill, when she lost sight of Eliza altogether.

Nowhere. She could spot Eliza nowhere. She ran to the rise in the road where she had seen Eliza only a moment before. Magen felt awkward and alone, and she was keenly aware of how much heavier her body had become. A kind of panic she hadn't felt since she was a child watching her father leave began to rise inside her. Her hands flew to her face distractedly. She heard a noise coming from inside the barn.

"Eliza!" Magen screamed. "Is that you?" Heading straight for the barn now, ignoring the hem of her shift gathering mud, Magen entered the barn's side door. "Aunt Eliza, answer me!"

A shadowed figure stood there facing her. Magen clutched her shawl squinting into the dark of the barn.

"What is it, Magen? What's happened?" Eliza walked toward her. Magen almost fainted with relief. The shadows lifted and the sunlight revealed her aunt walking straight and steadfastly toward her, but with concern etched in her face. "Magen, is it time? What is it, child? Let's get you inside."

Magen grabbed her aunt's arm. Exhaling loudly and holding her swollen middle, she tried to sound composed. "No. I'm fine. Really. It's just I thought I saw you out in the road. You were making your way toward me, but you would not return my wave."

Eliza stopped and looked at Magen. "You've just been working too hard. You're tired and overemotional. Let's get you back in the house."

The next few days were busy with the herd and field preparation. Because of the cold snap, they were behind with the planting, and Magen knew this concerned all the farmers. While she helped with what fieldwork she could, Magen was self-conscious about her appearance and mostly heeded Eliza's advice to work indoors on the sewing and on preparations for "the coming event"—as everyone now referred to the impending birth of her child.

Magen put great effort these days into holding onto her resolve and inner peace. She was more determined than ever not to let unnameable fears take hold. No matter how many times she replayed the events of that unsettling morning, or how many times Eliza assured her it was simply a function of being overtired, Magen still couldn't account for the vision she had of her aunt—no more than she could forget it.

Chapter 33

Out of Our Hands

Inspecting the kitchen garden one morning under a chilly gray sky, Magen was dismayed to see its slow progress. None of the herbs or vegetables had matured over the last week, and it worried her. She settled on filling her basket with the dried ginger and mint leaves hanging in the small drying cupboard off the kitchen. She would use these to brew a tea that would help with the nausea that still plagued her.

She watched the house for signs of Eliza. She knew Eliza planned to go to the far north pastures today to check on the herd that grazed there. These were the pastures she leased from the Reynolds family. Eliza usually stayed to visit with Louise whenever she made the trek out there, and Magen had prepared a journey cake as a surprise for Eliza to take with her. The morning was chilly so far and they were all back in their heavy woolen clothes.

She had overheard Eliza and Avery talking last night long after she had retired to bed by the hearth. She avoided the stairs altogether these days. They were discussing how their herds were going to fare if the weather didn't turn soon. The sheep had been sheared and could no longer fight the unseasonably cold weather with their thin coats of wool. Magen wished she could accompany her aunt today out to the pastures that were more than two miles away, but even if Eliza allowed it, Magen's condition would only slow her down.

Magen decided to head into the house and prepare something hot for Eliza to eat before she left. The pot of stew that perpetually hung from the big crane in the hearth had taken on a flavor of pork and sage today. Magen dusted the flat bread with a bit of oat flour and scooped out some of the aromatic stew on top of it just as Eliza walked into the kitchen.

"That smells wonderful. A bit of that will help take the chill out of the air. I just can't believe the calendar these days—us still fighting the cold."

"It's so strange! Hard to believe we're in June, and we're back in our woolens. You'll visit with Louise after checking on the herds?"

"I'll stop to visit if there's time. I would like to hear how it goes with them. If this weather doesn't change soon, our corn fields will fail to yield enough even for our small herd this year. What will they do with their sizable herds?"

"I made you a bit of cake that I'll put in your saddlebag. You may get hungry later."

"That's dear of you. But this stew will tide me over until I get back. I'll just finish my tea and be on my way. Avery will be back before sundown, I should think—save the cake for him. He's gone to see Clem Jamison about the plow." On her way out, Eliza grabbed the muslin cloak that hung in the front hall. "Surely the worst of this weather will be behind us soon. It's summer, after all. We all need a respite, especially the animals."

Magen helped her with her cloak. Then, from the kitchen window, she watched her aunt ride out on Betsy, the aging mare. The house was cold, and Magen longed to take her sewing out to the front porch, but she knew the chill would make it uncomfortable. Magen pulled her chair up close to the hearth where there was just enough light to do the small stitching the baby blanket required. Jane and Emmy had gone home for a visit, so she had the house to herself. She decided to try and enjoy the quiet, if not the warmth of the day.

For the next couple of hours, she labored over the blanket and listened to the small fire popping in the hearth. As it got later, and she got drowsier, she decided to go out to the barn to see if perhaps Avery had returned. Walking down the slope to the barn, she was alarmed to see the unmistakable signs of a snow sky. The air had a definite bite to it, and she pulled her cloak tighter. Avery hadn't returned, so Magen checked on the heifer and her new calf. They seemed happy enough in each other's company. After watching them awhile, Magen decided to return to the warmth of the kitchen.

As she left the barn she was astonished to see snow falling. She wished either Avery or Eliza would return. It was probably too soon for Eliza, but it was getting colder and this didn't appear to be just a snow shower. Feeling vulnerable and worried, Magen went back to the kitchen and began unnecessary preparations for supper.

Finally, at dusk, Avery rode up the drive in the wagon, which was weighted down with tools. Magen ran out to greet him. By this time the snow had accumulated to perhaps five or six inches. When Magen told Avery of Eliza's decision to check on the north pasture that morning, he looked alarmed. Seeing that Magen was even more alarmed than he, he tried reassuring her that Eliza could look after herself. Then he insisted that she go into the house and see to his supper instead of catching cold in the snow.

They soon sat over hot bowls of the savory stew that Magen had prepared for Eliza, along with baked apples in sauce. Avery and Magen discussed the bizarre weather.

"Some folks in town can't quite decide if the weather is a punishment from God or the work of the devil," Avery said.

"Punishment for what?" Magen wondered aloud.

"Folks always believe in the sins of others, Magen," he said with a twinkle in his eye. "I won't be telling Eliza this. Nothing gets her worked up quite so much as the godliness others see in themselves but perpetually miss in others."

Magen smiled, *They know each other pretty well, Eliza and Avery.*

"I'm sure Eliza is having a grand visit with Louise right now," Avery said, trying to calm Magen's fears and his own.

"Yes, she said she would stop off to see the Reynolds' if there was time and light enough." Magen looked out the window at the accumulating snow; there was no break in the cloud cover to suggest the snow would stop anytime soon. "Why don't we walk a bit toward the north pasture to see if she's coming up the road. Perhaps Betsy got injured, and she's taking it slow. We can take the big lantern."

"Lass, your aunt would never forgive me if I let you go out in weather like this. I'll unhitch the wagon and take the horse," Avery said, patting her hand with his rough one. While Avery went for his hat and great coat again, Magen went to fetch the lantern for him. She knew she would slow him down, so she didn't insist on going with him. They opened the front door and a whoosh of wind blew a heavy sheet of snow on them both. Pushing against it, Avery yelled to Magen that he would be back soon, "Not to worry!"

The grandfather clock in the parlor soon chimed the eight o'clock hour, and Magen stood to look out the front window for movement. The world was out of sync, she thought. *Could it be a punishment from God?* No. That was only Sara's voice that scratched her memory at anxious times. Chilled and shivering, she went back into the kitchen once again and pulled her chair up to the window to sit and wait.

Just past nine Magen jerked awake. She was stiff and sore from sitting in the chair, but she had heard something. Looking out the window she saw a light in the distance. She went for her cloak, wrapped it around herself, and headed out the front door. The snow was still falling, but slower now. It looked to be more than a foot on the ground with drifts alongside the road being shifted around by the howling wind. She tried to move swiftly, but her cumbersome body was unsure of itself in the snow. The ground was slick, so she forced herself to slow down. She made her way toward the road. When she got closer to the light, she saw Avery walking up the drive holding the lantern. She was winded by the time she reached him.

Magen took the lantern from Avery's hand. She could see the exhaustion plain in his face. "Let me help you," she said, taking his arm in her free hand.

"Is she back?" he barked out with desperate hope.

"No! Did you not see her? How far did you go?" Magen tried to keep the hysteria from her voice.

"I made it to the end of the north boundary, but the snow was coming down hard and I kept slipping into drifts that pulled me down. I called and I called, Magen. But nothing can be heard over that wind. I could not see her anywhere, nor Betsy. I made it to the Reynolds', but she had stopped there only briefly. Louise wanted me to stay, but I told her I had to come home thinking surely I'd find Eliza back here by now."

When they entered the house, Magen ran to get Avery a cup of strong hot coffee. He moved as if his joints ached, pulling off his snow-laden cloak at the front door before coming to warm himself by the fire. Magen pulled the chair she had been sitting in next to the hearth and instructed Avery to sit while she dished out some supper for him.

"The wind. The snow, so deep," he mumbled as if to himself. "What's going on, lass? How could this be happening?" Avery's brogue was getting more pronounced in his exhaustion.

"There's nothing more we can do tonight, Avery," Magen said. She was worried about the gray cast to his complexion. "I'm glad you made it back. At first light we'll be able to find her. I'm sure of it."

Chapter 34

Eliza Found

For the next few hours Magen paced the floor, either looking out the front window or going out to the front porch to peer into the dark, hoping to see the light from Eliza's lantern making its way toward home. And still it snowed. Avery had drifted off while sitting in the chair next to the fire. His boots were still on, his hat next to his hand. She pulled the cot closer to him and sat down on it. The next thing she knew she was being woken by the crow of a rooster. Avery was already up preparing coffee.

"There will be daylight enough now, Magen. The snow has stopped. There are about two feet out there. The animals will be in a state. I'm heading out again to look for Eliza. This time I'll take the northwest route. Maybe she wanted to check the grain troughs and took that road back instead." Avery said all of this without once looking up from the task at hand, his head shaking in disbelief.

"I'll see to the animals, Avery. And I'll keep the pot of coffee hot for when you and Eliza return," Magen said, kissing his rough windburned cheek.

Avery left, and Magen went to put more clothes on before heading out to the barn. Keeping busy would help she thought, and certainly there was enough to do. The two field hands staying at the farm just now would take care of the herds in the east meadow, but she hoped there was someone close by to assist her with the animals in the barn. She didn't know how they were going to manage; she wasn't capable of much physical work at this point. She could see to the chickens and feed the pigs, but the rest would have to wait.

After three more long hours of worry and waiting, Magen spotted Avery coming up the road at last. This time, though, she could see that he was on foot and was leading his horse up the snowbound road. The horse had a bundle of some kind strapped to its back that Magen couldn't make out.

Making her way down to him, to her shock, she could just make out that the bundle was a body draped over the horse's back. She couldn't breathe, she felt dizzy. But she made herself go forward, at last reaching the weary Avery.

"Is she...?"

"Just alive, lass."

They led the horse up to the house. Avery picked Eliza up in his arms and took her in. He looked as though he, too, was on his last legs, but somehow he managed. Magen cleared off the little bed next to the kitchen fire, which she stoked again. She pulled back Eliza's frozen cloak and shawl from her bloodless face.

"I searched and searched and saw nothing for the longest time, Magen," Avery spoke in a halting voice. "As I turned around to retrace my steps, I happened to spot something in the distance. A piece of her cloak blowing in the wind caught my eye. The snow was too deep for the horse to get through. Eventually I reached the spot on foot. She was buried in the snow, Magen. No sign of Betsy."

"Does she have a chance?" Magen's question sounded as desperate as the expression he wore.

"She's a strong woman, lass. But she's always had a bit of a weak chest and she's been through an unearthly night."

"I'll try and get something warm inside her," Magen said, now moving with a purpose.

Returning with a mug of hot plain broth, Magen felt a dreadful fear grow inside her. Eliza was feverish. She had a dry cough and labored breathing. Her eyes stayed closed. The woman who seemed indomitable yesterday now looked fragile. Avery went for more blankets and returned with a couple of heated stones; he slid them under the covers near Eliza's feet. He touched her temple and made soothing sounds under his breath.

For the rest of that day, the two nursed her. When darkness fell Magen persuaded Avery into lying down in the bed Eliza usually slept in. He was completely done in. But he made Magen promise that she would wake him if there was any change. Magen pulled in one of the wingback chairs from the parlor and placed it next to Eliza's bed. There she sat for the rest of that night, wide awake, holding her aunt's hand and willing her with every ounce of her being to survive.

When dawn broke on the restless household, the two had already been up for some time replacing the strong concoction of herbs for a plaster. Magen was boiling water for tea and seeing to the food for Avery. Eliza's appearance remained unchanged. After a few bites to eat, Avery said he was going for the physician in Saint Rock.

"She should be responding by now," he said. "No doubt the Doc will be busy with this weather, but I'll find him, Magen. I promise."

Magen held on to Eliza's motionless hand. Her coughing increased now. Although her eyes would open, it was like she was in a delirium and didn't recognize Magen. The quiet of the house began to close in on Magen. Getting impatient with her physical awkwardness, Magen heaved herself out of the chair to raise the blanket that hung over one window. As much as she didn't want to see the snow, the darkness depressed her more. Her body was stiff and achy. All she could hear was the steady tick of the grandfather clock and the deep rattle in Eliza's chest. As she looked out the window on the freshly fallen snow she remembered how Carrie sounded just before she died.

She lifted Eliza's head to try and get a tiny bit of broth past the cracked and parched lips. She adjusted the plaster on her chest to shift the congestion, and then sponged her skin with a tea of sage leaves to ease the fever. There was so little else she could do. Now and then Eliza would groan softly, her eyelids would flutter, and Magen would think she was coming around. But she didn't rouse, and her color remained gray.

After what seemed like an eternity, Avery returned with John Phelon, the physician from Saint Rock. Phelon was an older man, with sparse white hair and a reserved manner. He had known Eliza and Samuel since childhood, and he didn't hesitate to come out to Creed Farm when Avery found him. He knew how tough Eliza was, and understood the urgency of her state. Magen could only guess what Avery had done to track him down in this weather.

Phelon went to Eliza, who seemed to be agitated now in her delirium. He asked Magen and Avery to wait in the other room while he made his examination. Soon, Phelon called Avery and Magen back in. Deep worry flashed across his face.

"It's pneumonia. Being out in that night has weakened her already weak lungs."

Magen was astonished. "I've never known Aunt Eliza to complain of her chest," she said. Avery and Phelon just gave each other a knowing look.

"There isn't anything more that I can do for her. Keep her comfortable. Get her to take some broth if you can. I'll check back soon, but I must go now. There are so many others to see to. I am very sorry," he said with tired, kind eyes. He saw himself to the door.

Some minutes after Dr. Phelon left, Avery said "She has always had strength enough for us all." Magen attempted to comfort him but couldn't stop her own tears.

That evening, with Magen and Avery sitting nearby, Eliza began to stir. They both jumped up and went to either side of her bed. Magen thought she saw a little color in Eliza's cheeks, and her eyes seemed to focus. She attempted a weak smile as Magen sat down next to her. Avery remained standing at her other side.

"Aunt Eliza, we've been so worried," Magen said, reaching for her hand.

"I tried to make it back," Eliza spoke haltingly, in a raspy voice. "Snow was so heavy, so wet. Betsy... poor thing."

"I couldn't find you, lass. You were you hiding from me!"

Eliza, like a blind person, reached out for Avery's hand. "You found me, old friend," she whispered before drifting off again.

"She'll sleep for the rest of the night now, Avery. I'll just make some fresh tea and sit up awhile. Why don't you go on to bed."

After a while, Avery did as he was told. He looked exhausted; Magen feared for his health as well. Magen saw to Eliza's bedside needs and then sat down next to her, settling in for another long evening. After an hour or so, Eliza attempted to open her eyes and reached out for Magen.

Magen went and held her hand. "Save your strength, Eliza. Sleep now. We'll talk in the morning."

The next morning Magen woke up to Eliza's coughing. The plasters she had replaced diligently were doing little good. Her aunt's breathing was hard to listen to—all rails and crackles. She sounded as if she were in pain; her skin was like fine parchment.

Magen put a cool compress on Eliza's burning head. "Shall I let the morning in, Aunt?"

Eliza tried to smile, so Magen went and pulled back the blanket she had rehung in the window last night. She went back to Eliza and, with surprising strength, her aunt grabbed her arm.

"Magen, Louise Reynolds will be sending someone to help you. A good woman. Her name is Molly. She knows about birthings," she said in a rasping voice. She gasped trying to get air into her lungs. "In the bureau are all the instructions for the farm. It belongs to you now. You and your child. Avery owns half the yield and can build a home here if he wants. But he knows this. The important thing is Creed Farm is your home, always. Do you understand, Magen?"

She seemed so determined to be heard that Magen held both her hands and assured her that she understood.

"I am sorry it's my time now, Magen. With your child coming, especially."

"Aunt Eliza, don't say that. You'll be fine! You must! I need you. Please don't leave me! You are all that I have left," Magen cried now. She suddenly felt like the small lost child she once had been.

"Nonsense, Magen," Eliza whispered with what strength she had left. "You have a world of love around you and strength enough for all. We don't get to choose our time to go. I have had an extraordinary life here. And I was blessed the day you came to me. Now you and Gabriel…raise your children here and watch them grow along with the farm."

Magen couldn't believe what she was hearing. Eliza was the strongest woman she had ever known; this couldn't be the end.

"Take some hot broth, Eliza," Magen said, reaching over for the bowl on the table. But just as she turned back to lift the spoon to her mouth, Eliza looked Magen in the eye, and the light there vanished.

"No!" Magen dropped the bowl on the floor and wrapped herself around Eliza—as if by holding on tight enough she could somehow keep the life force from leaving Eliza's body.

Avery came running in from the other room, stopped short when he saw Eliza's face, and sank down into the chair. Neither he nor Magen spoke another word.

Chapter 35
Letting Go

For the next twenty-four hours Magen felt numb disbelief, and had momentary but devastating stabbing pains of sorrow. Nothing she nor Avery could say to themselves or each other eased the pain of missing Eliza.

At first Avery was angry. He couldn't get past the bizarre reality of how Eliza died. There had been other casualties of the snowstorm. But, as he saw it, Eliza should not have been one of them. Magen, too, was unable to make sense of the loss. And yet, hadn't she already learned the capricious nature of life?

Louise and George Reynolds had gotten word from Doc Phelon, and they came to Creed Farm the day after Eliza died. Dazed with grief, Louise explained that she had seen Eliza for a brief moment during the storm. Eliza had stopped in on her way to the north pasture, just long enough to ensure that Louise would be sending Molly over in time for Magen's delivery. Louise said she had reassured Eliza, but was unsuccessful in coaxing Eliza into the house. Eliza was convinced the snowstorm would soon blow over. She had assured Louise that she would just check on the herd and be home before dark. Before Louise could go in and retrieve a cloak to join her friend, Eliza was gone—snow covering her tracks as quickly as she had made them.

Louise had been worried as well about her husband George, who had been out working in the west pasture since that morning. She set up vigil in her kitchen that evening, just as Magen was doing at Creed Farm. As fate would have it, George Reynolds had also been stranded out in the snow that night. He took shelter under a feeding trough with his horse and made it back home the next morning, never realizing that his friend Eliza was dying less than a mile away.

Louise, Jane, and Emmy closed themselves into the kitchen to prepare Eliza's body for burial. George and Avery went to see about making a coffin. Magen chose the spot up on her knoll for Eliza's gravesite. There, Eliza's spirit would continue to watch over Creed Farm.

Two days after her death, the small group of friends gathered at the knoll, which overlooked her life's work, and said goodbye to Eliza Creed. *It was just as she would have wanted it,* Magen thought as they all walked back through the wind and the cold to the warmth of Eliza's kitchen. Much later, Magen would have a hard time even remembering the sequence of events of those first few days following Eliza's death.

Inconceivable as it was, life continued. And it continued without mercy—the farm demanded their attention and their labor. Perhaps that actually *was* mercy, Magen pondered one night as she gazed up at the moonless sky and a swath of brilliant stars. She and Avery had taken to sitting together on the porch after chores were done and some semblance of a meal had been eaten. Magen realized rightly this was the hardest time of day for Avery. This had always been the time he and Eliza shared together.

"I think that Aunt Eliza had always been surprised at her good fortune, Avery," Magen said, still gazing at the heavens. "The life she got to live here on the farm? I don't think, for one moment, she took it for granted."

Avery acknowledged this with a painful sound from deep within his chest, released, like always, in a puff of pipe smoke.

Chapter 36
Molly

The cold weather had changed over to an unseasonable cool. No more snow fell, but remnants of the unnatural storm were still evident in shaded patches and hillsides. Avery took off for a brief trip north with a few other farmers from the area to see about seed corn reserves. Magen was spending a quiet two days inside—the chore boys doing most of the outside work—when Molly arrived at Creed Farm.

Although Molly had but a few belongings, George Reynolds delivered her over in his buckboard. "I've got no time to stay, Magen. I'm off to meet up with Avery and the others. This here is Molly. Eliza and Louise sent her to help ya." And with that introduction George was gone.

Molly, who seemed to have only the one name, was a surprise to Magen. It had been mentioned that she had experience as a healer, so Magen had expected a much older woman, but as Molly had stepped away from the wagon, Magen guessed perhaps she was only in her early thirties. She seemed to glow with some inner delight. Being dropped off at a stranger's house to live did not appear to fluster her in the least. She was shorter and sturdier than Magen, and had dark skin. Her eyes were a goldish brown and penetrating. She was no stranger to hard work, Magen thought, as she watched Molly reach down and pick up a heavily-stuffed cloth bag with little effort.

Magen waved goodbye to George Reynolds as he urged his two horses on, and then felt shy and awkward. "I'll help you settle in, if you like. You'll be sleeping in Aunt Eliza's room," she said, feeling the terrible oddness of those words. "Shall I carry the other bag for you?"

"Of the two of us," Molly said matter-of-factly, "I think I best be doing the lifting and carrying." She bent to pick up the other, smaller bag with her free hand, and Magen self-consciously ran her hand over her extended belly.

"Looks like your baby will be making its appearance before too much longer. Another month, maybe?" Molly nodded toward Magen's midsection.

Magen was startled at hearing the subject brought up at all, and was even more surprised at the ease in which Molly stared openly at her large belly. "Well, I'm not sure. But I believe I might expect my confinement to come in August or September."

"Well, gracious lady! Let's hope your calculations are as precise as your speech." Molly said, laughing with genuine kindness in her eyes.

"Sorry. I wasn't meaning to sound grand. I'm just not accustomed to talking about...well, you know, the birth."

Molly put both bags in one hand now, and took Magen's arm in the other. "Then I expect you'll be needing a good chat," she said, and she headed them both toward the house.

Magen showed Molly Eliza's now sterile-looking room and left her to get settled while she put the kettle on. She felt her spirits lighten fixing tea for the two of them. She hadn't seen Avery in a few days and although there were the hired hands who all looked after her, she had been lonely. Molly didn't take but a few minutes to settle her things into Eliza's room. Before they sat down to tea, Magen showed her around the house and found herself beginning to chatter, which is what she always did when she was nervous. She didn't know what to do with her hands, so she stuffed them in her apron pockets. She felt strange being the lady of the house and trying to make this woman feel at home. She felt as though she were playing a part, going through the motions.

"It was Eliza that made this place a home," Magen said, thinking out loud. "I can show you the farm though, if you would like."

"Let's enjoy this fine tea you've prepared for us first."

The two of them sat at the walnut trestle table that Magen had loved sitting at when they were all here together, Eliza, Avery, she and Gabriel. Now the house seemed cavernous in its emptiness. Molly sipped her tea as she stared at Magen. Magen sipped her tea as she avoided staring at Molly.

"Miss Creed's man—he lives in one of the outbuildings?" she asked Magen.

"Avery was not her man. I mean, Avery and Eliza were friends. Together, they built up the farm. He sleeps out there, yes. He'll be back tomorrow, I think." Magen pointed out the window to the outbuilding where Avery kept his room in the back. "But he eats and lives in here with us though."

"And did he love her?" Molly asked calmly.

After some hesitation, Magen nodded yes. "They were the best of friends." She looked out the window at the building where Avery slept, and her heart ached for him.

"Perhaps you could show me the farm now."

"Of course. I'd like to," Magen said, relieved at given something specific to do.

⌒⊙

It still did not feel like the month of June. Both Magen and Molly had warm woolen shawls around their shoulders as they walked. Magen took note of the stillness that surrounded them. It was unusual for this time of the year. She felt better when Molly took her by the arm in companionable silence. The two women began to walk down the road, then crossed over behind the barns and into the fields. Taking in all of Creed Farm—the hills, the trees, the sky—Magen's sadness began to ease.

She began to point things out to Molly: "The shed there in Eliza's herb garden is where Eliza liked to sit and go over the house and farm accounts. She planted that cluster of white birch trees to hide the fish in that small pond from the blue heron that visits each spring. The beautiful new barn here is a testament to Avery and Gabe's fine craftsmanship." The more she showed Molly of Creed Farm, the more calm and whole Magen began to feel. It was as if the farm was breathing life back into her and the baby, who kicked the whole time they walked.

"If the animals are going to be fed next winter, that cornfield is going to have to grow fast and steady from now on," Molly said.

"Avery said some people think this weather marks the end of days," Magen said. "What do you think about it?"

"I don't know about this God people around here fear so, Magen. Nature itself is a great force. Let's just do what we can to live with what's in front of us without trying to figure out all that we can't see."

"Eliza told me you were a healer. You seem too young to be a healer."

"My mother was a healer among the Abenakis, and she taught me what she knew."

"What happened to your mother?" Magen asked.

"About ten years ago, the smallpox came upon the Abenakis who were wintering just north of here. They had never seen this sickness before. They called it the "hoggamog," or the devil. My mother took care of them, but her cures were not powerful enough to fight the sickness. She went to visit the healers in the Odanak tribe, kin to the Abenaki, to see if they could help her find a stronger medicine. She took the sickness herself and never made it back to us."

"And your father? Is he still alive?" Magen asked.

"With my Pa, it's harder to say. His people were originally from Africa. He was a slave and ran away from a tobacco plantation in the Carolinas. He came north to live as a free man among the Abenakis. One day he went down to the river to fish and a band of white men came riding through. We heard they took him with them. I haven't seen him from that day to this."

Magen was shocked. "Couldn't you do anything about it?"

"They were white men," was Molly's only reply. "But then you know the hurt of a father who's gone. Mrs. Reynolds told me about yours," she added. "That knoll above the fields there. Is that where your aunt rests now?"

Magen looked toward the knoll, again feeling that sharp stab of sorrow at her center. She looked into Molly's penetrating eyes and felt as though Molly saw right through to the inside of her heart. It was unsettling.

"Yes. I chose that spot to bury her," Magen said.

"She'll be able to keep an eye on the place, won't she? How about we go up and visit Miss Creed?"

Magen wasn't sure she was ready to go up there yet. She hesitated, but Molly pulled her gently by the hand.

"It's nice you got the chance to say your goodbyes to your Aunt Eliza, Magen. That knoll up there will be a place of comfort for you from now on."

Magen followed Molly up to the knoll. When they reached the grave, Molly said looking out across the farm, "You did pick a fine spot for her to rest."

"It's my favorite place on the farm," Magen said, casting her eyes everywhere but on the freshly dug grave.

After standing there awhile, Molly said, "I'll go and see to supper. You come along when you're ready."

Feeling alone and vulnerable, Magen watched Molly walk down the hill back toward the house. As her form disappeared, Magen turned toward the grave. In place of a wooden cross, Avery had carved a tiny bird on a twig ready to take flight. It was a simple thing and Magen liked the dignity of it. She knew Eliza would approve. For quite awhile Magen just stood next to the grave, trying to let the knowledge of all that had happened sink in. Magen remembered when she and Gabriel first arrived at the farm. It was less than a year ago now, but felt like more than a lifetime. How relieved she had been to be accepted by Eliza and to find a home here. *Now it's back to being alone again.*

The pain of it made her physically ache. But she didn't wish it away this time. This time she felt a kick from the baby—a less than subtle reminder that it wasn't just her now at all; she had her child. Wrapping her arms around her swollen belly, Magen reminded herself that she also had Molly and Avery. And someday soon, Magen was sure, Gabriel would be back. But even more importantly, Magen realized, she had what was right in front of her. She had Creed Farm to love and care for.

Chapter 37

A Different Place

As the days passed, Magen and Molly worked their way into new routines. At first Molly pitched in to help Jane and Emmy do the washing, weaving, mending, and general house chores, and Magen saw to the cooking. But even this eventually became too much for Magen; the large pots became heavier and the long hours on her feet became more difficult. She began to heed Molly's advice to take short naps throughout the day.

Avery, on the other hand, was slower to adjust to life without Eliza. He worked himself hard from sunup to sundown and often into the wee hours of the night. Sometimes when Magen came upon him while he was at work, he looked as though he were about to say something. She would detect that brief disorientation in his eyes at seeing her instead of Eliza, and then the fleeting look of pain that replaced it. It broke her heart.

"I wonder how long it will be before we have our old Avery back," Magen said to Molly as they were finishing their morning tea. "I don't think he turned in until awful late last night. I worry his health will fail."

"He's a strong man, Magen. And I doubt he has much choice in how to grieve for Eliza. We pretty much make that part up as we go along. I expect Avery will make his way back to us when he is ready."

As Magen became heavier and slower, she found herself content to stay close to the hearth and to Molly. Molly had a forceful character like Aunt Eliza, but she had a serenity about her that was comforting. She was not afraid of showing her vulnerable side, which made her more approachable as well. She never chattered, but spoke on many topics with a knowledge seemingly beyond her years. She knew the best way to slaughter a cow, or birth a lamb. She knew about the diseases people caught and how to tell a serious one from one that would not kill. She seemed to grasp the importance of any given situation, and never wasted time on frivolous things. But there was one thing Magen knew more about than Molly, and that was the love between a man and a woman. Molly hadn't yet met a man she esteemed so well, but she was curious about romantic love.

She asked Magen once how it felt to love a man. Magen tried to find the right words to express her feelings for Gabriel, but she didn't want to sound silly or trite. She finally settled on the words: "Loving Gabriel is like learning who I am in this world. He bears witness to my life. As I do his."

This explanation seemed to make sense to Molly, and Magen was grateful that Molly did not question Gabe's absence. Molly never made Magen feel immature or foolish. The two women were at home with one another. Molly's only concern, ever, seemed to be for the health and safety of Magen and her baby.

Best of all, Magen appreciated Molly's laugh. It came from somewhere deep inside her and made everyone around her feel good just to hear it. Deeply grateful for Molly's friendship, Magen soon came to think of her as Aunt Eliza's parting gift. With Molly's validation, Magen began to take on more and more of the responsibilities of being the owner of Creed Farm.

Avery accepted Magen as the head of Creed Farm with no apparent difficulty. Without any awkwardness, he began to consult with her about when to move the herd and what supplies to order. He gave her detailed reports of the effects the abnormal weather was having on the crops. He began to talk through things they might try in the way of damage control. He and Molly's unwavering belief in her cultivated a confidence in Magen that began to show. Both Magen and Avery were working through their grief by keeping Creed Farm afloat.

When she had time alone, though, Magen found herself yearning for Gabriel and questioning his continued absence. She had so much she wanted to share with him—about Eliza, about the coming baby, about herself. Sometimes the need consumed her and shook her fragile new foundations. Molly and Avery seemed to sense these times and never allowed her to flounder alone for long.

As head of household now, Magen knew she couldn't malinger. Daily, she made a mental promise that she would not dwell on what she did not have. Eliza was gone for good, and Gabriel would make his way back to her—or not. Life was filled with uncertainty; this she had come to learn well. All she had at this moment was the child growing in her belly and the desperate struggle to keep Creed Farm going.

As food and resources became ever more scarce, it was up to Magen to figure out how to stretch what little they had into an unknowable future. She took inventory again and again, then rationed, apportioned, and parceled off what they could afford to give to the village needy and to the more desperate farms.

As Magen became the true head of Creed Farm, Molly became Avery's "right hand" out in the field with the herd. And it wasn't long before Avery began to linger again after an evening meal. He'd sit on the porch with them for a smoke and a chat. On occasion, he even reminisced about Scotland when Molly showed an interest. Magen knew he was beginning to heal at last.

⌒☉

"You should have joined us! Saint Rock's Independence Day celebration was perhaps not as raucous as in years past," Molly told Magen, who had opted out of attending, "But folks made an effort."

"Usually the town wouldn't think of celebrating until after the haymaking," Avery said. "But this year, the fields are fallow. Not enough good weather to make a proper harvest."

"But the country's no longer at war," Molly said, determined not to have her spirits dampened. "And hard times can't last forever. Vermonters tried to look ahead to better days today, Avery. As should we."

"Of course you're right, lass," Avery said. "There's no one to blame for this 'abominable weather,' as it's now referred to. No government to curse, no unpopular politician to oust. The good people of Vermont must bide their time and do their best to survive until nature or the fates decide to change course."

Molly described the day's events for Magen: "The militia marched on the green and there were arms displays, even a rally of fireworks to entertain the children. It was a good diversion, with sorghum cakes for the young'ns and enough ale for the men. The women formed a quilting circle to get some work done—and gossip, of course. It was good to see folks together for a change, trying to have a good time and ignoring the worry in each other's eyes."

The respite of that summer day was short lived. Not long after the July Fourth celebrations, Magen and Molly discovered a terrible white mold on what few edible crops were growing in the field. And still the killing frosts came, late into the summer. The root vegetables that should help see them through winter were thin and spindly. The corn was small and green. Rainfall had been minimal since the snowstorm in June, and the temperatures were still unseasonably cold. Instead of harvesting from the meager pickings in the kitchen garden, Magen had been feeding the household from her stash of dried goods from the larder and kitchen attic.

This was the time of year for stockpiling—putting foods by to prepare for the long winter ahead—but this year Magen had to put the household on strict rationings. She wondered if her measures would go far enough. Avery had been telling her that the local farmers' attempt at a second planting had not proved efficacious because of the lack of rain and the continued frosts.

The predator attacks on the sheep that had plagued them throughout the winter were increasing now at an alarming rate. Molly mentioned that, according to the Abenaki, early winter was the usual time for the Wolf Moon. Yet it had been this month's full moon in July when the worst of the howlings echoed through the hills.

Late July and early August experienced more hard frosts. Where before there was grave concern, now outright fear and panic began to take over. Avery spent more of his time in town, because there was less and less work to do on the farm. He wanted to keep abreast of what folks were saying and doing. So far the sheep at Creed Farm were holding their own, but their feed crop dwindled. Their placid behavior, Avery feared, would not last through the winter.

On edge, the people of Saint Rock listened daily for the church bells to ring; this was their call to meeting, a gathering of neighbors to air concerns and discuss options. Magen wondered how Gabriel and his family fared in Bellingham. People in Saint Rock had heard that some areas had been unaffected by the freak snowstorm in June, so she hoped for the best. The families of Saint Rock farmers, to a man, had a pretty good understanding of the shortages ahead, according to Avery. He got an earful with every trip he made into town. In the evenings now, after they shared a bite to eat, he would sit at the table with whatever newspapers and bulletins he could get his hands on and read them to Magen and Molly.

One evening after listening to Avery's news, Molly said in a clear low voice, "It's the hunger time."

Avery looked questioningly at her, so she explained. "My mother used to tell me of times like these. Times when all of nature seems to be testing its people—no food, sickness, death, and fear all around. Everyone brought to their knees… only the strongest ever get back up."

After a bit, Avery said, "That would be us, lass."

156

Chapter 38

Continuity

Magen wanted Creed Farm to survive now as much for Avery's and Molly's sakes as for her and her child's. Molly had Eliza's energy but had nothing to prove as Eliza did, so she offered an ever nuturing presence that the whole household benefitted from. Magen desperately wanted Creed Farm to survive now for all of them. It was August now and the air still had a bite to it. Magen wondered if it would ever be warm again.

Going downstairs one morning she found Molly and Avery standing on the porch talking to a couple of men she recognized from Saint Rock.

"Magen, there are folks in town who are in need of Molly's doctoring and some food," Avery said to her as she walked outside to greet them.

"They are staying in the meeting house. There is talk of a fever," Molly said with an unspoken fear in her eyes.

"You both must go and see what you can do," Magen assured them. "I'll be fine. Don't worry about me."

"These men are helping out at the Reynolds' place. They'll get word to Louise to come and stay with you," Molly explained, holding Magen's hand.

"I'll be fine, Molly. Louise doesn't need to come. Emmy is gone, but Jane will be back soon. So go now, and don't worry about me. I'll get your bag of medicines for you." She saw them off, assuring them both that she would avoid strenuous work and would stay inside with her feet up. They, in turn, assured her they would return in two days' time, at the most. Magen smiled at Avery, hoping to ease the deep furrow in his brow.

Magen put her woolen shawl on and went out to the barn to look in on the animals. The fresh air, regardless of the chill, always helped to revive her. Moving slowly and deliberately, she looked in on Pinetop. She snuggled up to his strong warm neck and enjoyed his reassuring nickering. In spite of her girth, she managed to clean out the better part of two stalls and haul in some oats for the horse. Diverted now by the needs of the farm, Magen made her way up to what had come to be called "Eliza's knoll."

She knelt down next to the wood carving at the gravesite. She paid her respects and sat in silence for awhile. Feeling uncomfortable in every position she tried, she stood up again with great effort. Arching backwards to relieve a stitch in her back, she felt a terrible spasm. It startled her in its intensity. She came down hard on her knees, then reached out to the grave marker for support. Her water burst as she let forth a yell.

It can't be. Not yet. Not now!

Aware for the first time of the increasing cold and the darkening sky, Magen realized in a haze of pain how close the sun was to the horizon. *How had she lost track of the time? And where was Jane?* She was so cold, and she didn't know when to expect the next pain. She had to make it back to the house, and she had to do it now.

Magen walked painstakingly back down the hill. She tried to see what lay on the path in front of her, but the daylight had faded. She could so easily fall, she thought, trying to keep down her panic. As she made her way forward, she searched the fields to see if anyone else was around. She saw no one and trudged on.

Arriving at the barn at last, she thought perhaps she could find a farmhand. Just as she approached the back of the outbuilding where Gabriel had kept his bunk, a loud clap of thunder with a bright, blinding light flashed overhead. Magen let out a scream. In a viselike grip of pain and raw fear, she pushed her way through the heavy door. Aware of Pinetop and the other horses snorting and whinnying in their stalls, she felt her way with trembling hands to find a lantern or candle to help light the way. The only response to her shouts for assistance were the plaintive sounds of the animals.

She made her way to the small room where Gabriel had once slept— where *they* had slept together one night a lifetime ago. Another agonizing contraction doubled her over. She squatted down, holding on to the end of the wooden frame of the cot. She let out a wail; she could feel the pressure of the child wanting to come out. What was she to do? Panic and pain coursed through her. But between the spasms, Magen was able to shove empty wooden crates under the head of the wooden cot. Holding onto the two headboards with both hands, with her feet propped against the foot boards of the cot, she was better able to bear down and assist the baby's outward journey when the next spasm hit.

After what felt like an impossibly long time, Magen felt the head of her baby crown. She ripped off her apron and placed it underneath her before another heavy push wrenched itself from her body. She remembered the small scissors she always kept in her apron pocket for snipping herbs. *She would need those to cut the baby's cord ...* That was her last coherent thought as her screams joined the loud crack of the storm battering the roof overhead.

Chapter 39

To Begin Again

That cold August night produced little rain. But continuous rumbles of thunder and flashes of lightning rolled over the hills of Creed Farm. Louise Reynolds arrived at the farm later the next day to find Magen asleep on the daybed in front of the kitchen hearth with her baby daughter in her arms. As it turned out, Jane had discovered Magen and the baby in the wee hours after the storm and had helped them both into the house.

Louise quickly instructed Jane to make tea and broth as she thoroughly checked on Magen and the baby's condition. Molly and Avery returned two days later to find Magen and the baby recovering under the territorial care of Louise and Jane.

It wasn't long before Avery and Molly were acting like doting grandparents. Appalled that they had missed the birth, they now stuck close to both mother and child. They urged Magen to have a long "lying-in." But Magen would have none of it. A couple of days after the birth, she was up cooking the morning meals and working on her basket of baby linens. Her daughter was kept within touching distance at all times. She may not have known all the correct ways of mothering a child, but the loving of her child came naturally enough.

With a keen sense of relief, Magen felt less handicapped by her awkward size, and began to feel more like her old self physically. She couldn't keep her eyes off of her baby girl. The tiny thing had a dark mat of hair and hands that fluttered in front of her as if feeling her way. Her dark, bright eyes were intent on making out her mother's face; they followed Magen as she moved about the room. Magen could not get enough of the soft cooing and gurgling sounds she made.

They referred to her as the "wee one," or "the babe," sometimes as "the little girl." Magen thought about this one afternoon as she sat nursing her daughter in front of the popping, kitchen fire. Everyone knew life was precarious for newborns, and right now the future was uncertain for everyone. But Magen somehow knew they were not going to lose this child. Her daughter was going to survive.

"It's time I gave my daughter a name," she announced at supper that evening. Molly, Avery, and Louise and George Reynolds were all seated around the walnut table. They looked at her tentatively, apprehension written on their worried faces. Magen felt an overwhelming love toward each one of them.

"Her name is Elizabeth. Elizabeth Creed. When Gabriel returns to us, we'll have a wedding and change our names together to Magen and Elizabeth Creed Thayer." As she claimed the name for her daughter, Magen felt the culmination of endings and beginnings. At the end of one chapter of her life she welcomed the beginning of the next.

Chapter 40

The Hunger Time

The topic on everyone's mind and lips was that—as had been true of June and July—the month of August also had killing frosts, and the drought continued as well. While Elizabeth was growing slowly on Magen's milk, Magen felt herself weaken and tire more easily from her own lack of food. She wondered how long this could last.

It was clear by early September that the farmers in the area would get no relief from their second and then third plantings, and people were becoming wild with worry. The inhabitants of Creed Farm could feel the hysteria that lurked just under the surface of everyday life. Still, they persevered.

Another killing frost came about mid-month, followed by severe, successive frosts. The corn and potato crops were dead.

"Herds as far north as Canada and as far south as Long Island Sound are going hungry," Avery read to them one evening from a newspaper.

At Creed Farm, Molly and Avery worked tirelessly out in the fields. They had their hands full. The animals that weren't outwardly sick were weakened by hunger. The crops, having been hand-watered from what little was left in the well, were still eroding from the hard frosts. There were no extra hands to help now. Those free of family attachments had left the area to try and find work in areas unaffected by the freakish weather. Those who had families and could not leave began to look for alternative ways to eat.

Large fishing seines were kept in the Missisquoi River north of Saint Rock, in the area where Molly's family once lived. With Avery's help, Molly assisted folks in town to arrange for a trade of maple sugar for fish with some of the Indian villages living along the river. It hadn't taken long for Molly's skills as a healer to become well known. Creed Farm saw more visitors looking for food or for medicine. They gave of everything they had, and worked three times as hard to give more.

The severity of the suffering in northern New England depended on location and available resources. It seemed the areas worst hit in Vermont were the towns and villages closest to the Canadian border. Some of the larger towns south of Saint Rock seemed to be faring a little better. Oats and oatmeal became the dietary staple in Saint Rock, and fear grew in direct proportion to the dwindling amounts of this commodity.

Magen heard talk of one man just east of them in Smithfield who, believing it was the end of the world, killed his wife and two children before taking his own life. Another family, Molly heard, had lost their five-year-old boy in the June snowstorm, only to find his body more than two weeks later amidst a dying crop of corn.

She knew what panic did to people. When the British soldiers had captured and burned Washington D.C. just two years earlier, the horrific tales of looting and torture that appeared in the small newspapers across the country would make her hair stand on end. Later, she had learned that many of the facts had been exaggerated. Magen held on to this now. She wanted to believe it wasn't as desperate as they were being told. Thoughts about Gabriel and his family began to haunt her.

She was determined to keep her own panic down for Elizabeth's sake, as Magen was keenly aware of how totally dependent her baby was on her for comfort, nourishment, and life itself. Never before had anyone's existence solely depended on her. Most of the time she felt up to the task—except in the early hours of the morning, when Elizabeth would wake her up with heart-tugging cries of hunger. Magen wondered how long her milk would hold out if she herself continued to go to bed hungry.

＊

October, at last, brought a return to more normal temperatures. The temperatures continued to be more seasonable on into late autumn, but drought conditions persisted. Forest fires had sprung up everywhere, and the air in the Vermont mountains was laden with smoke and ash.

One afternoon, Molly turned to Magen who was working in the field with Elizabeth strapped to her back. Avery was tending a small ewe nearby. Squinting into the smoke-filled air, Molly said, "No one's heard of a wolf attack in days. Have you noticed?"

"They've moved on, haven't they, lass?" Avery said with a shrug. "This air's not fit for man nor beast."

"These times will pass, Avery, and we'll endure. Someone once reminded me how extraordinary it all is," she said. She took hold of Elizabeth's tiny hand. "I don't want to lose sight of that."

Avery gave one of his slow grins, knowing Magen was referring to Eliza. Looking first at Magen, then over at Molly, he said, "I think we've got to get these beasts and ourselves through a tough winter ahead, lasses, but you're right, Magen. We'll see the new year in. And next year, no doubt, we'll not be remembering our hollow bellies."

Chapter 41

The Homecoming

Avery followed through over the next few weeks, eking out the barest of livings for them all. When the corn supplies dwindled to nothing and there were no lambs fit to be slaughtered, he showed Magen and Molly how to scrape the inner bark of the giant white birch and grind it down to a starchy substance to feed to what was left of the hungry herd.

"It might be just enough to keep a few from starving," he said in such a way that everyone believed him.

The horses and oxen were too weak to be of much help around the farm, so the wood for the winter's fires had to be cut, chopped, and dragged out of the forest on the strength of Avery's back. So many of their hired hands had left, and Magen worried about Avery's health. She had asked George and Louise Reynolds to come and stay at Creed Farm, but George refused to give up on his own herds.

As the fall of 1816 turned into winter, many Vermonters did give up. Some just abandoned their farms, others headed out to the "Promise Land" of Ohio, or traveled further south.

The ugly side to humanity sometimes reared its head. They heard that in the southern part of the state men sold seed corn at inflationary prices to those in the north. But then there were the folks in New Hampshire who sent wagon loads of goods to Vermonters, expecting nothing in return, and Canadians who delivered food, blankets, and offers of assistance over the border without being asked.

People in Saint Rock began to make potash again to barter for food and goods with the Canadians. The potash trade had been common enough in Magen's grandparents' day. It required the cutting and burning of trees then leaching the ashes into lye. Once it had been discovered that sodium could be used instead of lye, the potash works had dried up, to be revived again in these times of need.

When asked by some of the townsfolk if the Creeds would let them cut a portion of the old growth forest on the farm's eastern ridge, Magen regretfully had to refuse. The giant hardwoods had stood sentry duty on Creed Farm for as long as memory. They were necessary to the farm's future, which was now her daughter's heritage. Magen felt she had no right to offer it away. So she offered instead the smaller grove of balsams and cedars, from which they could produce oils and medicinals. This proved to be a workable solution. In addition, Magen donated a supply of maple sugar that her neighbors used for barter with people in New York. The bees in the Creed Farm skeps managed to produce a good harvest of honey, which was traded for chickens and grains from farms further south. As in other hard times, it was neighbor relying on neighbor that got them through each day.

Eventually, and at long last, the forest fires were doused by late November rains. The rains did much to boost the sagging hopes of the ragged people. Reports of the end of the world and God's wrath were heard less and less. While the harvest was all but nonexistent in many parts of the northeast, early December saw somewhat milder temperatures, and this gave people what they needed more than anything else—hope.

Gathering and collecting the very last of the late autumn berries one afternoon, Magen hummed a lullaby to baby Elizabeth, who was tied onto her back with a strip of muslin. She took a moment from her gathering and untied her daughter to hold her in her arms. She never tired of looking at Elizabeth's rosy cheeks and shining curious eyes—in them she saw Gabriel. A great fear washed over her. Still no word from Gabriel, nor any rumors about his family.

Elizabeth gurgled, content in her mother's arms. *Eliza would have loved you so!* Magen thought.

That's what life is, Magen knew, as she watched her baby intently. *An incredible gift of joys and sorrows. The joys give us love and hope, and the sorrows give us wisdom. Sometimes a terrible wisdom.*

She hoisted Elizabeth's sturdy little body back into the cloth sack, shifted the baby's weight, and turned toward the garden gate. And there he stood.

Gabriel looked older, thinner, and tired. He stared at her and the baby with those deep-set, green eyes—filled now with unshed tears. Magen's voice caught in her throat. Elizabeth looked over her shoulder at him; she gurgled and cooed.

Magen held her breath, and tried to smile at him. Elizabeth's little hands fluttererd outward. Gabriel pushed through the gate and walked toward her. The hunger Magen saw in his eyes must surely be matched by her own. But this was a hunger of the spirit—both of their spirits had been waiting for so long.

His strong, rough hand took Magen's and touched Elizabeth's soft, pink cheek. There was no question of who this child belonged to—she had Magen's smile with Gabriel's deep green eyes. He unwrapped the muslin and held the baby in his arms, looking at her with a mixture of love and incredulity. Magen took a step back and looked on them both with a full heart.

"We just buried my mother. I came as soon as I got Adele on her way. I didn't know," his eyes indicated Elizabeth. "Why didn't you tell me?" he asked with an edge to his voice.

Magen put her hand gently over his lips. "Gabe, we did what we had to do. Now we can live up to the pledge we once made to one another, and now to our daughter, too."

"I'll never leave you again, Mae Creed."

"Mae Creed Thayer," Magen smiled. "And this is Elizabeth Creed Thayer … and we'll never let you leave."

Acknowledgments

My sincere thanks to the Vermont State Historical Library and Museum for cherishing Vermont's past, and to the historical museum in Milton, Vermont where I first learned of "the cold year" from a community quilt hanging on a wall. Also, my humble appreciation to all of the helpful librarians who aided me along the way. Any errors in historical fact in The Hunger Year are mine and mine alone.

Although writing is done in solitude, I am deeply grateful for the following people:

To Tess McRedmond Mohan, whose steadfast enthusiasm and encouragement for this story and all my writing over the years has meant more to me than she'll ever know.

To members of the Jeffersonville Writers' Critique Group: Moira Donovan, Sara Lee, and Kathleen Schwartz, whose friendship, humor, and talent I have enjoyed and benefitted from.

To Amy Cook and Greg VanBuiten for their friendship and endorsement of my work from the start.

To all those who graciously read earlier versions of this story and offered their observations and feedback—especially Sally Clinard—my sister and promoter, who read many and offered much.

To Lorraine C. Manley for the generous use of her beautiful art which graces the cover.

To members of the Hinesburg Children's Writers' Critique Group, whose experience and knowledge helped further my story even though my time with them was short.

And especially to my daughter, Mae, whose gentle nature and inner strength I attributed to the character of Magen Creed—and could then easily see how everything in the book might have happened.

References

I relied on many works of scholarship to learn about this fascinating time in our country's history. Here is a list of a few of them. Visit your local library to learn more.

Bacon, Richard M., *The Forgotten Arts* (1978)

Dodge, Bertha S., *Tales of Vermont Ways and People* (1977)

Everest, Allan S., *The War of 1812 in the Champlain Valley* (1981)

Fagan, Brian, *The Little Ice Age—How Climate Made History 1300-1850* (2000)

Fisher, Dorothy Canfield, *Vermont Tradition* (1953)

Hemenway, Abby, *Vermont* (1972)

Hill, Ralph Nading, *Yankee Kingdom, Vermont and New Hampshire* (1960)

Kelly, Catherine, E., *In the New England Fashion, Reshaping Women's Lives in the Nineteenth Century* (1999)

Krout, John A., *United States to 1877* (1966)

Ludlum, David, *The New England Weather Book* (1976) and *The Vermont Weather Book* (1985)

McCutcheon, Marc, *Everyday Life in the 1800s* (1993)

Nylander, Jane, C., *Our Own Snug Fireside* (1993)

Russell, Howard S., *A Long, Deep Furrow, Three Centuries of Farming in New England* (1982)

CPSIA information can be obtained at www.ICGtesting.com
Printed in the USA
BVOW01s2344290114

343003BV00004B/21/P